To Sam,

Embrace The Weird!

Not Before Bed

CRAIG HALLAM

Inspired **Q**uill Publishing

Published by Inspired Quill: December 2014

First Edition

Chief Editor: Fiona Campbell
Cover Design by: Charley Hall
Typeset in Adobe Garamond Pro

Paperback ISBN: 978-1-908600-34-9
eBook ISBN: 978-1-908600-35-6
Print Edition
Printed in the United Kingdom
1 2 3 4 5 6 7 8 9 10

Inspired Quill Publishing, UK
Business Reg. No. 7592847
http://www.inspired-quill.com

Dedication

For Laura
Without her, these stories would never
have existed

A note from the Author

Hello, Reader.

I like you already. You've glanced at the cover, perhaps read the blurb, and you've opened up this book to see what it's all about. That shows curiosity, imagination, and even a little bravery. I can see we're going to get on.

I've been fascinated with Speculative Fiction for as long as I can remember, which means I was probably fascinated before that. And as long as that has been happening, I've been drawn to the shadows. Nothing rocks my socks more than a creeping spectre, a questing tentacle in the dark. Poe and Lovecraft are my Gods.

And that's what got me started with these stories.

It all began with *Upon Waking*, a story that I literally scribbled down longhand in a manner that the title suggests. And after being encouraged by my partner, Laura (who will actually be my wife by the time you read this), to submit the story to the British Fantasy Society, I was hooked.

I am an addict, and I am not ashamed.

Author Crack is my drug (also known by the street names Scribbler's Ruin, Screw The Day Job, and Insomnia Dust), and it gives me a rush from every idea, every new chapter, every *The End*. When I'm denied it, I'm cranky to say the least. If you should ever find me in this state, there are two ways to handle it; either lay me down and whisper snatches of Poe until I start to suck my thumb, or throw a notepad and pen from a safe distance and wait until my eyes have glazed over. It will then be safe to approach.

What you're about to read is the result of being on that drug. It is not pretty. It may lead to a fretful sleep. But it certainly has been fun.

I hope to see you hovering over another of my pages in the near future.

Embrace the Weird, my friends.

Craig Hallam (2013)

Laughter on the Landing

IT WAS PERFECT. With light spilling in from the enormous windows and its open plan layout, the apartment was just what I'd been looking for. It was a little cold, but that was to be expected. A dilapidated warehouse on London Wharf had been refurbished into a trio of apartments; partly because they were listed as buildings of interest, partly because the housing situation in our not-so-fair capital had reached breaking point. Still, it was overlooking the river, separate from the other buildings in the area and that suited me. The light and isolation would work wonders for my writing.

The sound of creaking floorboards tracked someone's movements on the floor above.

"Oh, that's the only real problem with this place," said the estate agent, who waved it away as if it were inconsequential. "A bit rickety on the floors. It's a young woman and her daughter upstairs. They don't make much noise and you probably won't see them. She stays at home to look after the little girl; she's quite sick. Shame really."

"What about downstairs?"

There was still another apartment below, or so I thought. I wanted to make sure that no hairy biker type was going to beat me up every time I walked to the loo.

"No one down there. Just storage," he said.

"The noise won't be a problem."

"I doubt you'll even notice it after a while," he said. He straightened up his frame, which just made his gut stick out further, and spread his arms to encompass the world.

"So, what do you think?"

"I'll take it."

I'VE NEVER BEEN so productive. Fingers rattled on keys like the clack of an old locomotive. The sun scuttled toward night like a beetle making for its hole and I realised that I hadn't eaten all day.

Stories and articles poured out onto my over-heating laptop, whizzed their way across the electronic postal service, and often returned with rejection emails attached. Still, I was happy and times seemed good.

The noises from the floor above didn't intrude on my concentration. In fact, they added to it. My previous apartment in the middle of Willesden had been terrible. The murmur of traffic and watching feet tramp by my below ground window had driven me to distraction. I was constantly aware of a world outside the front door and it dragged me away from the places I created in words. But here on the wharf, I felt as if the whole world were empty, uninteresting, and that my laptop contained all the characters I needed.

The sounds from above worked their magic. I felt as if I weren't alone while having the place to myself. Sometimes, after lunch (if I remembered to have it) I would lay and listen to footsteps and murmurs of speech, imagining what they were doing up there. I felt like a mortal eavesdropping on the affairs of gods.

A young woman and her little girl, the estate agent had said. I pictured them in my head, forging them into stereotypes. I generally avoided them in my writing but liked to indulge when not working. How can you break the rules and stretch the stereotype if you don't acknowledge their existence? And so the woman who lived above me was slightly smaller than myself, slender with childbearing hips, her brown hair tied into a loose ponytail as she washed the dishes at the sun-streaming window. She looked down with adoration at the little girl making shapes with some of her mother's left over pastry.

Standing on a chair to reach the kitchen table, flour dappled the oversized apron which hung down below the girl's feet. The white powder smeared her face, a ruddy glow beneath. The very visage of domestic bliss. Except there was no father figure. No one for the little girl to run to when they came home from work.

My mind turned.

The girl lay in bed; that was why I never heard the softer footsteps of a child above me. Hair clung to her glistening brow in serpentine strands and her eyes were heavy like tomb lids. I fought to regain the previous sunshine image, but couldn't. Distressed, I swung my legs off the couch. I had to rein in my imagination. It had a tendency to sabotage me at a whim. A foul taste rose in my mouth, as if left by the swiftly declining dream. I didn't know what they were really like but the little girl's image haunted me for the rest of the day; her ashen face and wistful movements, tiny limbs tired from the sickness. It blocked my writing, and I soon gave up entirely.

Daytime television: the nearest thing to oblivion we mortals can achieve while still breathing. Slumped in front of the screen, I tried to forget. Time and again the small girl's sallow skin rose before my eyes, and something struck me.

For the next few days, I applied progressively sinister explanations to the noises above and harnessed them. Fashioning the darkest tales I have ever written, the cryptic noises fuelled the darkest, most disturbing reaches of my imagination.

Tortured souls kicked their feet across naked floorboards as they were dragged helplessly by fiends. Things with no name and no face bumped and jostled in the pitch abyss over my head. The mysterious apartment above my own became a fountain of terror.

The tales I wrote were my best yet and I secretly thanked the noises when I received my first magazine acceptance. Then I set the dark tales aside. During the course of my writing, I had managed to scare myself and needed to return to lighter material before I was tortured by my own imagination.

STRANGE HOW THE brain eventually brushes away something that was once so tangible as to cause genuine, though illogical, fear. The upstairs noises had been driven into the background of my mind and I barely noticed them unless I wanted to.

I still hadn't met the only other inhabitants of my building and wasn't particularly bothered about pursuing it. Knowing that the woman upstairs was home all the time, she would no doubt know that I was too. I didn't want her dropping in for tea and biscuits at every opportunity and dislodging my concentration. I know, that's extremely selfish but remember that I took this apartment for the peace, not camaraderie.

However, it seemed fate that I meet the woman upstairs.

I was busily typing, giving myself square eyes and a healthy little migraine, when the thump came. So sudden and heavy was the sound that I swear I felt it in the boards beneath my own feet. Having been engrossed in my work, I didn't know if it was the first sudden sound. It could have been the third or fourth for all I knew. Stopping dead in mid-sentence, I held my breath, waited to see whether there would be another.

My imagination went into that familiar over-drive. There was something about this apartment that always made me think the worst, like an itch at the back of the brain. What if the little girl had collapsed, or her mother had slipped in the shower? Suddenly, I became aware that I was the only human being who could be roused for assistance if something horrible happened on the floor above. I was halfway to the door before I realised that I had reacted at all. Sheer instinct had driven me across my apartment. Whoever said that humans are cruel by their very nature would have choked on their words if they'd seen me.

I admit, as I bounded up the wide stairs, I felt somewhat heroic. As I banged on the door images swept past me of how I could react to any situation that presented itself, highly sharpened and blindingly fast from the adrenalin. When she answered in perfect calm, I ground to a halt like a juggernaut stopping for a bunny rabbit.

"Can I help you?" she said. She stood in the narrowest gap between door and jamb, dressed in what appeared to be a workout outfit. I compared my imagined image of the woman upstairs to the reality. Her hair was blonde where I had pictured brunette, she was muscular and obviously worked out rather than the typical mother figure my mind portrayed.

Stood there on the landing, sweating like a lunatic, I felt such an idiot. She looked petrified – and rightly so. After all, in her doorway stood a stranger in bare feet, a pair of ancient jeans and t-shirt, sweating and panting. No wonder she was dubious. I must have looked like a psychotic hobo.

"Erm…" I began, pathetically. "I heard a noise, downstairs, and just wondered if you were ok."

"Oh," she said. And didn't offer much else. She simply looked me up and down.

"Sorry," I said, unsure of what else to say.

"Don't be, it's…sweet. You just look a little-"

"Mental?"

"A little," she said.

She smiled behind her hand as if she didn't want me to see a crooked tooth. I noticed an old wound, a scratch on her bare forearm. Maybe she had a cat. There were many things I didn't know about this woman, that was obviously one of them. She had probably bought it for the girl. A pet for the sick child. I hoped that the animal didn't scratch at her too.

"Well, I won't pester you for a cup of sugar or anything. As long as you're ok."

I turned away, aware that I'd just made a terrible neighbour joke, and started down the stairs. She called from behind me:

"Thank you!"

"No problem. I hope your daughter feels better soon." A stupid thing to say. I knew the girl had been ill for a long while. What were the chances of her getting better from something like that?

I heard the faint sound of the woman catching her breath. I had said the wrong thing. Idiot. Her door clicked closed as I reached my own landing.

That's why I write. I'm no good at talking. My internal monologue is excellent but when it comes to speaking, especially to pretty neighbours, I'm lost. I cursed myself for idiocy for the next few days and remained vigilant for sounds of distress from the floor above.

✖

THE LITTLE GIRL I never saw, but after my embarrassing flight up the stairs, I saw Jennifer more and more.

The lid of the bin shut with a bang and I turned to find her behind me, a large bag of refuse in either hand. It was strange to see her in the sun and her complexion almost completely reflected the light. She spent far too much time inside. I offered to take the bags for her and she let me, even though she was clearly capable of doing it herself. The muscles in her arms put mine to shame. When I lifted the bags, they were heavier than she made them look.

She smiled sweetly, always covering her mouth like a giggling school girl. She was pretty, but I found myself completely uninterested. Maybe she had too much baggage, maybe my life was too busy (as I always told myself), or maybe it was the fact that I knew I'd never stand a chance with someone like her. She was out of my league, even with the emotional baggage and social isolation that must come with a chronically sick child.

"How is she?" I asked, as I always did. I felt it appropriate to let her know that other people cared what happened to her daughter. I'm afraid I'm painfully observant at times, or maybe I pry without realising it. Anyway, I'd never seen Jenny and her daughter receive visitors. Only the old man who delivered her shopping on a Thursday. There was no sign of a significant other, no grandparents and no friends. I lived a similar way, preferring my own company, but I didn't have a sick child to care for.

"Not too bad," she said. "She's eaten something at least."

"That's a good sign," I said, trying to placate her with obvious statements. In my defence, my medical experience was restricted to putting on plasters and using antibacterial hand wash. All I knew was that eating was good, not eating was bad.

She didn't answer, but gave a tight-lipped smile. We walked back into the building together and I watched her climb the stairs to her tower; Rapunzel trapped by the love for her child.

I don't like to admit it, but I hoped for a swift end for the girl then. I stood in the brick and wood hallway, in broad daylight, and hoped that a child would die peacefully and swiftly for the sake of her mother. I have never gotten over the sensation of self-disgust that came swiftly after, no matter how much I try to tell myself that it is natural to have such thoughts. Everyone who has ever nursed a sick relative must have felt the same, no matter how fleeting. I wondered if Jenny had. I instantly tried to take it back and hoped that no demons were listening in on my mind, waiting for an errant selfish wish to grant.

THE SOUNDS FROM Jenny's apartment became a reason for me to visit. I know what I said earlier, but that was before I met her. Now, I felt compelled to give her just a little break, even for five minutes. Just to let her see another human face was my only intention. I certainly never stepped over the threshold. Standing on the landing, Jenny tucked into the gap in her doorway, we would pass the time of day under the pretence that I was checking on her safety. The noises were various in style and volume. Some were a scraping sound, as if of heavy padded objects being moved, obviously furniture being moved; some were thuds as a chair was replaced, or a can of beans were dropped. Often there were voices, which I always attributed to television since I never saw anyone come and go. I would bound up the stairs (the only exercise I ever took) and rap jauntily at the door. Sometimes she would already be waiting for me. After a while I began sharing my theories on what the sounds were, trying to make them funny or elaborate to amuse her. She would always smile and give a perfectly rational cause for everything, explaining away every knock and bump, and I would pretend to be a dolt, slapping my forehead and rolling my eyes. We had quite the skit going. It could have gone on stage.

I was never invited in and I never wanted to. We were just fine laughing on the landing.

WEDNESDAYS WERE MY day off. I don't know why I

chose that day rather than the typical Sunday, but I did. Maybe it was so that I could go out when everything was open for business, just so that I wouldn't waste my day.

On this particular Wednesday I sat on my couch, feet up on the coffee table, and sipped my coffee. As a rule I don't read books while I'm writing. If I enjoy the style of the novel I find it creeping in to my own work. I'd hate to be sued for plagiarism; I can't afford it. So, I was reading the newspaper. It's alright to only read it once a week; the same vital stories are rewritten a hundred times in a week anyway, so I never worry I'll miss anything.

A sound unfamiliar to me caught my ear. It descended as always through the creaking boards that made my ceiling. Anxiety gripped me and I set aside my paper to listen. The sound was a voice. Low and rumbling, much different from Jenny's mid range murmur. It was unmistakably male. I knew it wasn't the television as it was directly above me. I had ascertained over the last few months that Jenny's television was over the other side of the room and it never made any other sound than the pops and whistles of children's shows. I set my thoughts aside, sure that it would just be the delivery man arriving a day early, and returned to my paper. Anyway, how would it look if Jenny had got herself a date and her nosey neighbour turned up?

I blocked out the voices and continued to read.

Scree scree scru scree: They moved to the kitchen.

Rrrrhhhum: The chair pulled out.

I couldn't help but hear.

Gumnghromnan: The man's voice.

Momonah: Jenny's.

Gruhm. Rorandhum?: He asked a question. There was a tone there that set me on edge. Not anger or violence. It sounded like surprise.

How could I be translating incoherent sounds? Was I *that* used to eavesdropping?

As I wondered, silence had fallen. They were quiet now. Maybe kissing. It would be nice if Jenny had found someone. She certainly needed it and my useless attempts at pseudo-friendship lacked a certain something.

Then a sound from inside my own apartment. If it hadn't been for the silence, I would never have heard it.

Poit.

I leant to see around my feet, which were still up on the coffee table.

A drip. A splotch of dark crimson on the oak surface. For a second, I watched it as if waiting for something to happen. It did. Another droplet fell in the same spot.

Plit.

Drawn upward, my eyes widened.

On the ceiling, a line of the same fluid had trickled before dripping. It was leaking through the floorboards in Jenny's apartment—

Before I knew, I was half way up the stairwell.

Not stopping for the door, I barged in, reeling when it didn't move as fast as I'd expected. Stumbling across the hallway, I almost fell into the living area and turned, ready to fight off Jenny's attacker.

The man sat at the table in his grey suit, his face pressed against the wood until it bent his nose out of shape, eyes staring blindly at the surface next to him as if spying on a line of ants. His skull was the wrong shape, and it oozed a viscous fluid onto the table top which ran to the edge and dribbled into a puddle on the floorboards.

"Jenny!" I yelled. The shock of seeing the stranger in such a state rooted me to the spot. I should go in and find her, make sure she's alright. But I couldn't move.

"Here," came a weak reply. I span about so fast that my eyes blurred and I thought I would pass out. Darting back through the hall, I made for the living room.

Whoever had designed our apartments had very different things in mind. This was obviously built for privacy where my own was intended for modern living. Jenny's apartment had doors and alcoves. Every room was entirely separate from the next. It was homely where mine was spacious; cosy where mine was cold.

On an old embroidered couch last in fashion in the 80s, her hands covered in scarlet spatters, sat Jenny.

I stepped forward, and stopped dead.

"Jenny, what ha-."

The words caught in my throat like wire.

In the corner of the room, beneath the window, was a cage. A large cage. The type you would buy for an unruly Rottweiler. Curled inside with the mesh casting crosshatch patterns on her hair and body was Jenny's daughter. She was sick, but not in the way I'd imagined. Blonde hair had been dirtied to brown in matted clumps and at first I thought she had been beaten bloody. Her face was sullied with stains and her fingernails were dark as if from burrowing.

She was eating.

The flaccid fingers of a dismembered hand hung from her dainty digits. She nibbled at a well-manicured finger delicately, like a squirrel with a taste for nail varnish.

The child looked up, still chewing on raw meat. Her eyes were so heavily bloodshot as to appear almost black, and colder than a killer's. Not a glimmer of childhood. If I didn't know better I would have said she was no more alive than the man sat at Jenny's kitchen table. The girl's clothing was torn as if she had lived under a bridge all her life, her teeth stained with dried blood. This feral child's existence seemed impossible to me. With her mother sat a few feet away, staring at her hands, I was certain that I was hallucinating.

I forced Jenny's name from my lips once more but received no answer.

With my trance broken at the sound of my own voice, I finally recoiled, forced myself back against the wall.

Jenny looked up at me. Her cheek was sprayed with a fine mist of blood from where she had turned her face away while attending to the stranger in the kitchen. Tears streamed down her face, contorted into a portrait of anguish.

She moved toward me, and I didn't run. I couldn't.

"Please," she said, her voice raw with crying. "She's alright. It's just when she gets hungry. She gets so hungry."

She reached out to me with her blood-plastered hand and I turned away from her pleading face.

With the child's dead eyes still on me, her mother growing closer, my voice released a desperate whisper.

"No."

I closed my eyes and waited for the sticky touch. None came. Whether through instinct or divine intervention, I threw myself to the side. Chunks of crumbling plaster peppered my face and hair. Dazed, I lashed out with my feet and Jenny fell awkwardly, the candlestick she'd been raising above her head sent skidding across the floor, clanging on the child's cage. The girl jumped but made no sound.

Jenny was gone and I didn't care where to. Shaking myself, half-blind from plaster dust and sweat, I scrambled toward the exit.

Her door, the one I had rapped on so many times, the one that I had never gained entry to, slammed hard in its jamb with me outside. With this physical barrier between me and the horror, I rested. My hand was slick against the handle and I rested my head on the wood for a moment to collect myself. Through the delirium of fear and onslaught of gruesome imagery, a single thought pierced. As if trying to maintain some semblance of normality, my brain said:

This would make a good story.

The door wrenched from my hand and I almost fell back across the threshold.

Jenny stood in the doorway.

The thin blade looked so comfortable in her hand. Yet she held it away from her side as if reluctant to acknowledge its existence.

"Please," she said again. "Don't run. She's just sick, that's all. I'm just trying to make her better."

I ran.

Fumbling down the stairs, my head wanting to travel faster than my feet.

Never has my mind been so focussed as when fleeing from that mortal danger. I raced out of my building, across the tarmac and down the empty road to the busier streets beyond. The world blurred as I sped through it. I don't remember steering my body in any particular direction. All I knew was that I had to escape.

Sitting almost casually on the bench in Haggerston Park, my body shuddered with exertion. I wept, I think, and thankfully no one stopped to ask me why. I would have lost my mind right there in the park if I'd had to recount what I had seen. I made my way to a police station, said only that there had been a murder and gave them the address. I wouldn't speak another word until they returned and I sat feeling utterly vulnerable in the cells for almost three hours.

THE AUTHORITIES FOUND nothing of Jenny or her daughter. Every item they owned had been left behind, as had the staring corpse. They blamed me at first, of course. The cage was gone and only when they found chains beneath the girl's bed did they begin to believe that she had existed at all. As evidence of Jenny's other victims was unearthed outside the building or stowed away in her apartment, I was slowly absolved.

After months of counselling and living in a hotel in Richmond, I returned to my apartment. They said it would be cathartic to face the scene. Still, I remained downstairs and wouldn't even cast my eyes upward to the place where I had laughed on the landing with my pretty neighbour. I feared that Jenny would be stood there, the girl peering from behind her leg like an ordinary child but with the eyes of a psychopath, despite what my common sense told me. If anything has come of this, I now know that common sense doesn't serve so well when faced with the uncommon. It had told me the woman who lived above me was telling the truth, that the noises from her apartment were innocent and not made by her victims in the throes of death. Common sense had lied to me, and our relationship ended messily.

I lived there for another three months in relative peace, if only to prove to myself that I could. No sounds filtered from above and I was comfortable in the silence. Only rarely did I think about the apartment, or about Jenny's blood-splattered hands, or of the gnawing sounds her daughter had made.

Then came the day for the new tenants to move in. As I understood it, they hadn't been told of the events upstairs. The whole thing had been kept relatively quiet when the police realised they would probably never find Jenny. I knew they were coming; the same estate agent who had sold me the apartment came to let me know.

I waited.

The pressure built inside me like a steam engine with no valve. I was driven to distraction. Pacing the floors, almost scratching at the walls, I waited.

They arrived with trucks full of furniture and cases full of clothes. I heard their voices, the squeak hinge of the door, and with the first *scree* of ill-fitting floorboards, I was gone.

Mandy in the Jar-O

AT FIRST, SHE panicked.

A thousand thoughts flooded her mind:

I'm drowning.

I'm dying.

Where am I?

I have to reach the surface!

Ouch!

Flailing her limbs against the water's drag, Mandy's elbow slammed into the side of the jar. The pain of a stricken funny bone brought her to her senses.

She wasn't drowning at all. The viscous fluid held her suspended, filling the narrow glass tube, warm and surprisingly comforting in its support. What she had mistaken for drowning was the fluid filling her lungs.

I'm a pickle!

Amanda Hargreaves realised that she was naked. The glow from the floor panel was unflattering, making a textured spectacle of her cellulite. Despite her unexplained suspension in the miraculous fluid, Amanda tried to gather her modesty.

Swiftly approaching her 30th year, Amanda had noticed a pooching at the stomach, which arrived unbidden and refused to leave. Her breasts, she thought, were looking sad; maybe it was from the lack of attention. Her reflex was to cover up. Legs crossed and knees raised, arms cupping her breasts, Amanda looked like a shy foetus. Her hair (which she now regretted not washing in case she were to be rescued) floated around her in a cloud of tangles. She flapped at it as if swatting midges to better see her surroundings.

Through the tube's distorting concavity, Amanda could see a room, or rather a gallery of sorts, which stretched away to an internal horizon in either direction. One wall, the opposite to her own, was lined with curved bulkheads, each one holding an equally curved window that stretched floor to ceiling. Stars drifted past as if space were on a conveyor belt. As she watched, the windows were slowly filled by a green-blue mist that broiled against the windows and then was gone.

That's a cool effect, she thought. *I wonder how they do that.*

Just when she was starting to think that something special, unique and magnificent could be happening in her life, she realised that she wasn't alone. To her right was another glass tube, another inhabitant. So, as usual, she was nothing special. Just another one of the herd.

Typical.

Her fellow captives were like nothing she'd ever seen. On the long, dateless nights when she had little to do but wallow in her loneliness Amanda had watched the Discovery Channel until she fell asleep, jealous of the beautiful and intricate mating rituals of the birds, the enthusiastic thrashing of the beasts in the throes of passion. The creatures in the adjacent jars were something that might appear in her Attenborough-inspired dreams; a mix of animals that may at first seem familiar but were warped by the fog of sleep into strange concoctions.

The creature to her right began to struggle as it woke, just as she had. It swiftly realised its predicament and began to swim around the jar quite happily, paddling with its long-toed paws.

Humph, said Amanda, annoyed that what appeared to be an Ewok/Sloth hybrid had caught on faster than she had.

The jar to her left was full of pale tubing that writhed and ground together like a host of albino eels. Amanda recoiled when the tubes snapped apart to reveal eyes, almond in shape and colour.

A barrage of imagery assaulted Amanda with

such force that her head was thrown against the tube's side.

So deep beneath the sea that Amanda thought she might catch the bends when she woke, the city clung to a rocky precipice, suspended above an impenetrably dark chasm. Everything was pitch darkness. She clicked and squeaked as she swam, navigating her surroundings by pulses of shimmering blue that she could hear rather than see. She could feel the tickle of algae on her stomach as she swam, her body lithe and fluid in its motion.

The coils of the squid-like creature snapped closed, bringing Mandy back to her own senses. For a moment, each finger was an anemone frond; her hair a tussle of seaweed; her eyes unnecessary in the dark. As the sensation faded, Amanda caught a rogue thought in the loose netting of her mind. Not a word, but a brain wave with intonation.

Captured. Zoo.

When she remembered how, she opened her eyes and jumped again. Outside her jar stood one of Them. The light from her tube penetrated it, as it had no skin, and lit the chemical inner workings of the Thing's anatomy. She was sure that it was peering in at her, even thought it had nothing to peer with.

Amanda had never felt such attentiveness.

She was a thing of beauty, a being to be beheld

simply for the joy of it. And above all humans, she had been chosen; collected. The Thing rocked and swayed slowly on the spot as if to unheard music. Was it dancing for her? Was it displaying its affection in the only way it knew how? Was this her mating dance?

Amanda believed that no man could ever fall in love with her in her current state of imperfection, and so she had resigned herself to a life of loneliness when no fad diet or celebrity exercise regime would rid her of her genetic shortcomings. According to her magazines, if you didn't have a husband by the time you were thirty, you weren't going to find one. And so Amanda was filled with hopeful love for this amorphous Thing. A creature such as that would have no concept of her impotent words, her clumsy body language, her stutters and stumbles. It wouldn't know if her perfume was too strong, or if her scarf didn't match. It would listen to the events of her day with fascination and would never expect sweaty, awkward sex in return.

She felt love like she had never felt it before: reciprocated.

With cautious fingers, she reached out, their tips paling as they pressed the glass, displaying small circles of compressed flesh to the Thing beyond. For a while, nothing happened. Then the Thing got the idea and raised a tentacle. Its flagella rippling and wriggling, the Thing caressed Amanda's tube with a trio of tentative suckers, separated from her own hand only by the glass. The swirling in her stomach (which may have been seen as revulsion by another), Amanda took as the spark of chemistry between them. Who was she to deny the attraction between two beings? Even if they weren't of the same species. How could she turn away such adoration when it was, above all else, what she craved? She basked in the affection of that unfelt touch...

Wait, she thought, *come back!*

Her Thing had tired of the charming glass-pointing trick and slithered toward the next jar where the Ewok/Sloth was swimming cute little somersaults. Amanda's brief moment of extraterrestrial romance was reduced to a silicate residue on the outside of her jar. At first she was mortified to be so easily cast aside. But, with determination rising like indigestion, she set her resolve.

She'd never been leader of a pack, thinking of herself more as the extra packaging; or ahead of the curve, as her curves were lumps; nor a player of the game because she was pretty certain that everyone was playing by different rules. But to be beaten to the punch by an alien Teddy Bear, *that* was insulting.

So, her Thing was fickle, it bored easily.

Alright, she thought, *see what you think of this.*

She began to flail her hands and feet, slowly

building momentum. Breasts trailing slightly behind her, her hair whirling in a slow-motion cyclone, Amanda twirled a watery pirouette.

The Thing wavered, and returned to her tube. Its flagella quivered and whipped the air like the flick of a cat's tail.

Does that mean you like it? she thought.

As Amanda span faster and faster the Thing's excitement grew. When its attention wavered, she changed her shape, or the direction of her spin. She would raise her arms like a ballerina, or her knee.

Yes, let me be your favourite, she thought. She felt pretty, exotic. She was happy to be the Thing's pet, content just to please it and be pleased by its pleasure.

But, soon enough, she grew tired. Her arms drooped and her head lolled. She fought to keep spinning, but her hair began to settle around her face as her momentum lessened. How long she had span for, she didn't know, but she had to sleep.

Whump.

The first jolt was more of a surprise than painful, but enough to rouse her. The Thing stood outside her tube, flaccid, disappointed.

Whump.

The light beneath her lit the fluid with a flash and the jolt came again. This time with pain setting nerves afire wherever the water touched her skin.

Amanda yelped, but the fluid stole the sound.

Wha-what's happening? she thought.

Pressing her hands against the tube's side, she worked her aching limbs back into a spin. Her feet flailed loosely, her poise was nothing like it had been.

Another jolt, stronger, and Amanda's spine spasmed. Her gritted teeth almost shattered from the force.

Please, please, I'm so tired.

Whump. The pain.

Please, no.

Whump. Amanda's eyes closed so tight that beads of blood began to form at the corners. Her body stiffened. She felt something snap but it was lost in the pain. Her chest was on fire.

Please...

The final thump of light, brighter than any before it, faded.

Amanda's body hung like an old rag, toes dragging on the tube's floor, spinning her this way and that with the flow of the fluid.

The Thing paused there, and then understood.

The tube's light flickered and died.

The Thing stayed, but only for a moment, to admire the reflections of fleeting stars that skittered across Amanda's motionless silhouette.

March of the Broken

UNSTEADILY I TAKE to my crippled feet, make my first shambling step.

Survey the carnage. The ground is slick with scarlet and I drag my reluctant toes through the gore, unsure of my destination. The silence is maddening. I can't feel myself as I move, propelled forward by preternatural will, but I can feel the hunger. It rises in my dulled mind with insatiable ferocity that catcalls and jeers to only me.

There are more, so many now. We move in shuffling unison, a broken battalion, an exodus of the hungry.

And there are the others. They move so swift, and always away.

Please. Don't leave me.

My voice sounds so morose and the words merge into a single hollow syllable. Some of them cover their ears as I plead in vain.

Only in the earliest morning has the city ever been so still. There is a dreadful tension in the chill air. The buildings themselves seem to quiver with the effort of remaining unnoticed. There is a vacuum caused by the holding of mortal breath as I wander by.

A sound. It catches my ear and I am drawn.

My tattered hands scratch ineffectually at their walls, their doors. They plead like prisoners afraid of their guards. They beg me to leave them alone. I can hear them from behind their barriers of brick and wood. They think them impenetrable. Nothing is more timeless than me. I am beyond the grasp of Time and Death. Neither your bricks, your wood, nor your fragile lives can withstand my patient hunger.

I wait. Outside.

There is a press of bodies without people. Torsos and limbs held together by force of habit. We jostle and sway in the dark, our senses strained toward one inescapable goal. There is movement and the mob flows with wilted vigour. A sorrowful lament rises from our swelling ranks.

I am here. Can you not see me? Help me.

Let me inside. I'm so alone and the world hurts my insomniac eyes.

Sometimes they shriek and writhe in my arms. They beat at me like a beast, thrash and struggle. The thick taste of tin as it jets against my palate or the wet crunch of flesh is all that I ask for. Yet they are so reluctant.

I just want to be warm.

I see you, a face from the locked vault of my mind. Your hair, I remember, felt as if I were touching a dream. I knew you before. There was something before the stained shirt. There was something before your face was so cold and scarred with tear tracks. You know me. Who am I now, that you see me with such loathing? There was love there once.

A whisper as you raise the rifle to your shoulder.

Yes. That was my name.

You say you're sorry.

Please, please.

Lovecraft

1

HE WASN'T MY first boyfriend, he was just the first sign that my standards had reached an all-time low. In the back of my mind, I called him Murphy. That's because he looked like Robocop without his helmet on. The other reason was that his feet were so cold he could have been built with a metal exoskeleton. Good for keeping my beer cool though.

The next "man" was Gory Greg. He thought the name was funny. I did the first few times, too. He was a graphic artist with a whole lot of determination but no talent. I stayed with him just long enough to point that out, and define for him why he never got anything published. Then I moved on.

I like to leave my men with something to ruminate on.

There were others. Men with enough facial piercings to make a metal detector melt down, or with beards intricately weaved into their chest hair. One thought that Brut was a viable alternative to bathing; another asked if I'd have twenty back piercings and lace it up with ribbon because he thought it would look cool. I'm sorry, but using my scapulae as a corset just doesn't appeal.

But I seem to be moaning. Let's skip to the part where I took the bullshit by the horns and changed my life.

After Murphy there seemed no hope of ever finding a decent upstanding man (who was just a little dangerous, to keep me interested). And trust me, without sounding like I'm easy, I'd been around. I'd like to say it was one of my female friends that gave me the idea that finally turned me around, but the truth is, I don't have any. I overheard a conversation in my local library.

Two girls, both wearing enough pink to make a marshmallow vomit, were giggling to themselves behind a book. Designer school bags, pencil cases covered in Tip-ex and Felt-tip love hearts, exercise books with their own first name (Chastity, which I doubted; Toni, note the I) and their crush's surnames repeated over and over in psychopathic mantra.

Get the picture?

Neither of these people should have been in a library. I doubt they could even spell the word. But beyond all belief and laws of the universe there they were.

The book they were "reading" wasn't quite big enough to conceal the glossy magazine behind it.

Just as I was wondering who had let either of these Muppet-esque characters into a house of knowledge, their inane conversation took a turn towards the interesting.

"Okay, so, you can, like, pick any guy in the *world*, and, you know, mix and match, type of thing. Which parts would make up your *perfect* man?" said one of them.

A man with a mental filter strong enough to sift out all of your pointless conjunctions so that actual human speech was left? I thought, but remained quiet, satisfied with my own smirk.

Let's skip how her friend answered because I fear the paper you now hold may spontaneously combust with pity for the state of the human gene pool. Suffice to say there was much giggling, and refer- ences to footballer's "packages". I always imagine that footballer's sperm would be whipped into an impotent milkshake by the sheer amount of unsup- ported jiggling. Or maybe that's just wishful thinking as it removes any hope of them procreating.

Anyway, the seed was sown, and I thought, why *can't* I make my own man?

A group I hung around with at the time had

what I thought to be the means. I'll admit, I was naïve. I thought that a chalk pentagram and black, cannabis-scented candles were the actual shit. As it turns out, they aren't. So I asked them, hypothetically of course, if it was possible to create a person using dark majik (the spelling only highlights how literacy and imagination shift in direct correlation to each other). They pointed me toward friends of theirs, and they to some of their own, until I stood in the opium soup of a post-modern mystic's den. It was just off the high street, shielded from the general public by a large blue dumpster.

The internal mustiness, I thought, added to the authenticity of the shop, and the fact that I could reach out and touch either wall with my finger tips seemed to feel right. The ancient hippy/goth behind the counter was of little use unless you needed a draught excluder, and so I searched the stacks myself. I must have been in there for days. It was like the T.A.R.D.I.S. if Doctor Who had been a kleptomaniac.

Beneath altar cloths made in Taiwan and moth-eaten boxes of damp incense sticks, after my jeans were covered in a patchwork of moulder, damp cobweb and dust, I found what I had been looking for. The book was the size of a novel, although thrice as thick. The cover may have been human skin, although I doubted it. Its clasp flicked open almost enthusiastically, and I'll admit a sense of trepidation tickled me. The writing inside may have been written in virgin's blood, or the ink was simply faded by time. On the inside cover, an inscription read:

> LONGE HAVE AYE TOILED AT THYS TRANSLAYSION.
> YOURE FRENDE, A. ALHAZRED

The rest of the book was in similar old English, never was a word spelled the same twice. As I thumbed the crackling pages, stomach-churning diagrams flicked past my eyes with thankful swiftness. The handwriting appeared to get worse as the book went on, until the final page was nothing but incoherent scrawl.

A small paper price tag attached to the clasp read only £3.00.

Perfect.

If I didn't find what I needed in here, then I wouldn't find it anywhere.

I've always prided myself on being sharp, but I'll admit that I never wondered why an ancient tome of such obvious delicacy was stored in a shop full of bongs and cannabis-motif paraphernalia. Or maybe I'm answering my own question. Still, it seems odd that it should be so easily found; like it wanted to be read.

The hippy/goth muttered something as I slipped

him three pounds-worth of ten pences (I'd bought a bottle of water from the newsstand around the corner and they had no pound coins). I ignored him, as I would a homeless man or a child, and left with the book tucked into my threadbare satchel.

2

THE INTERNET IS a beautiful thing.

Although it may be full of writhing, sweaty human bodies for the most part, it also gives the layperson access to items that would be impossible to find elsewhere. The Internet, it seems, is the perfect tool for the modern mystic.

The book sat on my bedside table for almost a month. I flicked through the pages, making notes of necessary ingredients, placing Post-Its in the pages I would need later. According to Mr. Alhazred, it *was* possible to conjure a person using ancient black majik. There were warnings and cautionary statements throughout the book, but nothing that a person used to Government Health bullshit and Gossip Mag diet advice couldn't handle.

Slowly but surely, the brown packages started to arrive.

Over a period of weeks I received heavily padded jars, wooden cases and sealed bags. Grave dirt, hanged-man's bones, cat eyes, and a skinny-fit black t-shirt that I'd spotted on eBay were all among the packages. It wasn't long before my arsenal of obscure occult items was laid out across the chequered linoleum in my kitchen. I had waited for night time, although the book didn't say I had to. Again, it just felt right. The flickering amber glow from the streetlamp bleeding through my blinds tried to kill the mood but I was too stoked to care.

Incantations and a mixture of the first ingredients.

My pestle and mortar ground dusty bones and grave dirt into a potent powder.

According to the book, I had to picture what it was that I was conjuring, or who. My perfect man. What *did* I want?

The physical image wasn't important, I told myself, although the brooding, dark character in my head said otherwise. He should be warm, romantic in a subtle way. He should need me as much as I needed him, to be cared for and loved. He should want me and only me; that was important. He should love doing what I loved to do. He should be undoubtedly cool, spontaneous, with a hint of danger.

I'd seen enough T.V. to read the incantations with, I thought, an authentic drone to my voice.

My skin crackled and crawled. I wasn't sure if I was imagining it or not. I hoped not.

Mr. Perfect was on his way.

Now came the pinch. My own blood in the mix. Self-harm comes easy to some, but not to me. I never understood what was so necessary about it. I'd seen kids, real young kids, who looked the part of the "alternative" loafing around the local shopping centre with deep scratches on their arms. It made me sad to think that the practice now defined our subculture. It made people afraid of us, misunderstand who we were and what we were after. Then again, when it gets down to it, many of the kids looked too young to understand themselves. I'd always found ice cream to be a far more apt way of de-stressing. Although when I think about it, scratches heal; my spare tyre never shifts.

A thin trickle of deep red dripped into the sacrificial bowl (99p from Wilkinsons). It was all I could force myself to spare, and that hurt more than enough.

I was expecting a rattle of doors, a preternatural wind to whirl around my flat, maybe the distant crackle of fiendish laughter. Some pyrotechnics would have been nice, or a column of smoke that folded in on itself and expanded until all that was left was Mr. Perfect.

Instead, I got:

phut

In between blinks, it had appeared without ceremony.

There was, however, such a stench of rotten eggs that it clung to the clothes and throat like cough syrup or the scent of an elderly aunt.

In the centre of the chalk pentagram, where my sexy dark stranger should have been, was a… Thing. The capital letter is definitely necessary. It was about the size of a bread bin, and had no body that I could make out.

I had conjured a ball of writhing tentacles flicking its fronds at the air. Between the tentacles were one or two rubbery tubes that opened and closed, or sucked with an odd sound like an octogenarian attacking a Werther's Original.

What had I created?

The book had warned that dealings with the black arts hardly ever conjured exactly what you asked for. I thought that was an obvious warning, like "may contain nuts" on a pack of macadamias. I have, after all, seen *The Craft*. I was sure that I'd at least end up with 70% of what I'd ordered. As it turns out, black majik is like shopping on QVC.

With no diabolical receipt or return to sender, no 0800 666 666 helpline to consult, I resigned myself to the fact that I was stuck with…It. With all of the phallic imagery going on in that little wriggling thing, I guessed it was male.

I picked it up at arm's length, feeling it hold onto my hands like a captured squid. Groaning under my breath, my step quickened as I moved across the kitchen.

Dropping into my kitchen sink, it looked so out of place beside my *CSI* mug that I laughed. Flicking on the kitchen light, all of the satanic trash was rendered just that. Moving back to the sink, I saw it properly for the first time.

It was actually quite cute, and a dusky grey-pink in colour. I turned on the tap and began to wash it, not knowing what else to do. It was covered in some kind of ash but soon came clean. It splashed and blew water out of its orifices like a child playing in the bath. I wondered if I should get it a toy boat or a welly-yellow duck for next time.

Clean and happy (or so I imagined dependent on the light chittering sound it made) I placed it on the table while I swept my black majik into a dustpan. I came back now and again to tickle a tentacle or tube, and it squickled and pooted whenever I did, pleased with my affections.

Kitchen clean, it was time to feed. Now came a true test of my ingenuity. What do you feed a demonic tentacle-spawn? Instead of trying to decide, I picked it up and carried it to the fridge, intending to let it decide for itself. With so little to choose from, it had a hard time deciding. A piece of Mild White Cheddar took its fancy, though. It searched the block with its prehensile suckers.

Back at the table, cut into chunks, the cheese was devoured enthusiastically. I figured that so much dairy wouldn't be good for his tubes, and vowed to go shopping the next day and bring back some experimental snacks. For now though, I was tired.

Digging out an old shoebox from my wardrobe, and quilting it with a tea towel, I set my new friend inside. As I stroked his waving fronds and cooed assurances, I was struck by inspiration.

I would call him Lovecraft.

3

DESPITE HIS LACK of limb, torso or face, Lovecraft really was everything I had asked for. He loved me as much as I came to love him. His tacky caress was always gentle and came without me needing to ask; he would be waiting in the hallway when I got home from work with a cuddle and a toot from his orifices. It was like being royalty and having my own little tuneless fanfare.

I often cooked him macaroni and cheese, one of his favourites, although I was never sure whether his snorting consumption of the pale tubes could be considered cannibalism.

We watched movies together. On his first viewing of *Evil Dead II*, he breeked and nickered along with the funny and the grotesque as I laughed and squirmed. We were inseparable, except for when I had to leave the flat, then I would always rush home to be with him again. My little Lovecraft, my little Tubular Bell.

I know, I know, I'm talking about a squid-beast from the nether realms of God-knows-where, but any dog or cat owner will tell you this: he didn't need conversation or facial expression to convey personality.

All I needed was Lovecraft.

Of course, I sometimes met men and brought them back to the flat. Some things Lovecraft couldn't provide, tender as he was toward me. A penis being one of them. He would sit in his box like a good boy until they were gone, and then we would watch *Who Wants to be a Millionaire* together. As Chris Tarrant read out the options, Lovecraft would blart at the answer he thought was right. He was surprisingly accurate most of the time. I doubt he would have made a very reliable phone-a-friend though.

In all the fun and affection, I had forgotten one of the criteria that I'd imposed on the ritual when conjuring Lovecraft. The final one. Danger. I'm a sucker for dangerous men. I know they make terrible boyfriends and last as long as curry in a Granny, but I can't help myself! The part of me that likes eyeliner, biker boots, and pale faces just attracts them.

Lovecraft showed no signs of being dangerous. Nothing had ever happened that would tip me off.

He had always remained hidden when anyone visited and never been violent. That was, until the Jehovah's Witness turned up. That poor bastard.

A jaunty knock took me to the door. At first I was unsure whether I was being addressed by an FBI agent or funeral director until he pressed the leaflet into my face.

"Have you been touched by the Lord Jesus Christ?" he asked as if he were commenting on the weather.

I don't mean to be offensive, but I've never taken lightly to any religion. Especially those that ram it down your throat. I have been known to stand beside a street preacher in Leeds town centre and join in. The sight of a young woman dressed in a *Rammstein* t-shirt enthusiastically agreeing at the top of her voice tends to put them off. I take my inspiration at these points from Eddie Murphy's Gospel-esque characters, clapping my hands and gesticulating wildly. I'm used to being stared at so it doesn't bother me. In fact, I often get quite a following.

But anyway, I was in no mood for the Jehovah's Witness at my door that day. He wasn't doing anything wrong, as such. He's just enthusiastic about his belief. Still, he took it a little far on the wrong day at the wrong door.

"Have you been touched by the Lord Jesus Christ?" he'd asked, and I replied.

"No, but the Holy Spirit gave me a love bite behind a bike shed once."

He never faltered, God bless him for that. He just ploughed right on through.

"My, what a lovely flat you have!"

And that was where he went wrong. Shoving me aside with a copy of *Watchtower*, he actually pushed past me and into the flat.

I was stunned. I'd always given these kind of folks a good five minutes or so of theological debate before thanking them and slowly closing the door. I'm not a monster. But this time he was having none of it.

He was in.

"Oh yes, very quaint."

Stood in my living room with a side-parting like a cyclone trail and shoes so shiny that Hubble could have picked them up from orbit, he commented on my décor. I felt like I'd walked into an episode of *To Buy or Not to Buy: God Edition*.

He started to talk. And man, could he talk. I don't think I picked up half of what was said, but the general gist got through. He must have seen my eyes glaze over and knew he had me, because he suddenly said:

"Can I have a glass of water?"

As if hypnotised by his stupid grin, I floated out of the living room.

This was where *I'd* made a mistake. You see, before the Witness had arrived, Lovecraft and I had been sat watching TV, and that faithful squirming ball still sat on the settee where I'd left him.

I turned the tap on too fast and the water rebounded from the glass's bottom, spraying me, the wall and the worktop.

"Shit!"

The tea towel made short work of the dribbles but I had to refill the glass more carefully. If I hadn't been so careless, if I hadn't taken so long, maybe I would have been in time to save the poor trespassing git that stood in my living room.

But I wasn't.

The glass, which was having a very bad day already, smashed on the living room floor, spraying water over my socks.

The Jehovah's Witness lay on the carpet, his shiny feet twitching like a dog in sleep. Lovecraft saw me seeing him, and deflated guiltily. The man's face was gone. I don't mean in a metaphorical sense, I mean there was a gaping hole where his blathering, grinning face had been. It was surprisingly neat.

"Oh my god," I said, rushing forward as if he might still be alive with such an obviously fatal injury. "Ohmygodohmygodohmygod."

Lovecraft backed away, a dog expecting the newspaper treatment.

"You killed him," was all I could say. I slumped back against the settee and buried my face in my hands, as if protecting it from a similar fate.

Lovecraft must have taken that as some kind of signal, because the sounds of crunching and slurping began.

I daren't look. I didn't want to see. The sounds were bad enough. I sat there and sobbed, listening to Lovecraft eat his suit-sealed meal. I sat until long after the sounds stopped, long after darkness fell outside.

4

AFTER THAT NIGHT, after I finally peeked from between my fingers, after I saw the empty suit sprawled on my living room floor by the light of my flickering TV set, nothing was the same.

Lovecraft was still himself, as loving and attentive as always. It was me who had changed. In my experience there comes a time in every relationship where you finally see something you didn't expect in your partner. A hint of selfishness perhaps, or of cruelty that changes the way you see them forever after. You still love them, maybe even more now that you have seen their flaw, but you're never the same. Your guard is up.

That was how it was with Lovecraft.

Outwardly there was no tension, but inside I was

afraid of who would be coming to the door next.

Please bear with me for a moment, because a lump still rises in my throat when I think of what happened next.

The day arrived when Lovecraft became ill. It started over a week before the final curtain, when he first turned away from his Dairylea Dunker. It was odd; I'd never known him to refuse food before. In fact, I was sure that he'd grown thicker of tentacle since I'd conjured him.

From there on, it was downhill.

I would wake in the morning to find him still in his box, rather than beside the bed where he invariably crept after I fell asleep. A blast of Nirvana or AC/DC no longer had him trumpeting tunelessly or propelling himself along the floor in his oddly excitable way. He became sluggish, as if always tired. Something laid heavy on him. It was like the Jehovah's Witness had given him chronic indigestion.

The final day, there was no denying it. Lovecraft was dying. I found him in the kitchen, bumping his tubes against the coffee table blindly, as if lost. His luscious pink had drained away to a porridge-grey. When I picked him up, he squirmed against my hand lovingly but with no real gusto.

There was nothing in Alhazred's book on how to nurse a sickening tentacle-pod. I was at a loss. The only thing I could think of was that his being in our mortal realm for so long, eating our food and watching our terrestrial television, was having the same effect as it did on humans; it was killing him. The final nail in the coffin had been the Jehovah's Witness.

Lovecraft had to go back. I'd known it since bundling that dead man's suit into a bin liner; since the night I'd spent listening to Lovecraft's satisfied grewping.

I scraped together the remaining ingredients from his conjuration and scoured the book for some exorcism that would return him home.

Sitting almost entirely still, Lovecraft's colour was not dissimilar to the chalk pentagram around him. The incantation was simple, repetitive.

Droning onward through my tears, I mentally said goodbye to my Lovecraft, the best man I had ever loved, who had never even needed to be a man. If truth be told, I would have selfishly held on to him if I could. But another part of me, not so deeply hidden, was grateful. Returning him to his home soil (or whatever they used for the ground where he was from) was the best thing I could do for him, and me, and I still loved him too much to watch him die.

The faint smell of rotting eggs had risen as if from my blocked drains. I didn't notice it until Lovecraft's colour began to return. A thin mist appeared from somewhere in the protective circle.

Lovecraft was re-inflating to his old bulbous self before my eyes.

The invocation slipped entirely from my mind. I reached forward, wanting to stroke my bundle of joyous squirming one last time.

There were no words, no goodbyes.

phut

In the time it took to blink aside my tears, Lovecraft was gone.

A high-pitched toot rang out from beyond the veil.

5

SOMETIMES I THINK that life has a basic form to which it always reverts. You might call it Mundane, or Boredom, you might call it simply Existing. Whatever it is, between moments of grief or elation that pique our interest, life always returns to this basic state.

Mine was no different.

I missed Lovecraft terribly for a while. I kept his box and his tea towel. I continued to buy macaroni cheese until it filled an entire cupboard in my kitchen. But my life continued and soon I could go days on end without thinking about him.

The book stayed on my bookshelf, wedged between *The Shining* and *Interview with the Vampire*. I almost forgot about it. Eventually, (on a day where I decided I would have to return the macaroni and cheese because I'd never eat it myself) I took the book down. It would have to go back too.

The shop was exactly the same. Smoke escaped the door as I stepped in, macaroni-filled bag swinging against my leg. There was the hippy/goth with his eyes like cranberries and whiskers of wire. Another punter stood at the counter. He fingered a Rastafarian figure and stuttered a lot.

"I was just wondering," he said. "Do you, um, do you have anything like...I don't know how to say this...magical?"

My ears pricked up. Alhazred's book seemed to squirm in my satchel. A new victim.

"I'm not getting you," droned Hippy/goth.

"You know, like magical. Spells and stuff."

The hippy/goth reached under the counter and produced a thin volume with a glistening laminated cover. He offered it to the punter.

"A book of love spells?"

"It's not got me laid yet, man, but you might have more luck," said Hippy/goth.

The punter stuttered before saying, "I was hoping for something a little more authentic."

My book squirmed again.

I stepped up beside him, removing the book from my satchel and placing it on the desk. The punter, turning to look at the volume, turned toward me too.

He was actually quite cute in an uncomfortable-in-his-skin kind of way. He shoved his glasses back up his nose slope and tried to smile. It was like watching lettuce go limp. He shrugged inside his leather jacket. Some bastard had told him he'd grow into it. He hadn't.

"Something like that!" he said and reached out.

I slid it away. It fell from the counter and landed with a rustle of bin liner.

"You don't need that," I said. "I don't suppose you like macaroni and cheese?"

"I-it, uh, it's my favourite," he managed.

I don't know what my look was. Maybe I looked at him with smoky, sensual eyes. Maybe I just looked at him too long, but his cheeks flushed as if slapped. He put his hands deep into his pockets and dropped his chin.

My hand stroked his freckles for a moment. He looked up at me with eyes that had seen too many Romero movies and not enough young women.

I stepped into his personal space like a chav begging for change.

"Gimme some sugar," I said.

I kissed him hard. I kissed him like Bruce Campbell.

It took a moment, but he got into it.

The hippy/goth slid the new-age bullshit book back toward himself, turning it over in his hands. He

thumbed the crisp pages, stroked the cover, and said:
"*Wow.*"

Upon Waking

IHAD A dream.

This wasn't the Martin Luther King type of dream. There was no humanity, no hope. I sat at this computer for the longest time before beginning to write, uncertain whether the words would appear on the screen if I began to type. That was the kind of dream I had.

The trainers I wore in the dream, threadbare and comfortable atrocities I use for my infrequent runs, are at my feet. I had to check that there was none of the slate-coloured ash on their soles when I woke this morning. That was the kind of dream I had.

I'm skipping ahead of myself. Let me start at the beginning, or at least at the beginning of the dream.

I strode through a landscape hideously alien to everything I've ever known, and yet was wracked with the deep pangs that come only from returning home after a long absence. Vast spires of black silicone scratched or pierced low-hanging thunder-clouds that folded in upon themselves in a silent maelstrom. They held the only colour I was to see in this place; a malevolent scarlet that tinged their rolling edges.

The ground was a charred desert. The faithful trainers I mentioned before kicked up clouds of heavy silt or ash that settled too fast for it to be either.

Unsure of the nature of this place, unsure of everything other than an innate sense of returning, I was reminded of a nocturnal sculpture park. Structures that may have been buildings cast unnerving silhouettes in my path. They could have been glass pillars of enormous girth, melted to amorphous masses by an unfathomable heat. Or maybe they were grown this way. That was the word that occurred to me; not built but grown. And something flickered inside. Not light, there was no natural light in this place, just a hanging luminescence that only highlighted the shadows. What moved inside these grotesque masses appeared fluid, like the grinding of an eel's coils in dark water.

I moved on, aware that my heart didn't pound or thrum in my ears. There was, however, a sensation of comfort, of belonging, that in itself chilled my core.

Through the melted monstrosities I strode with the confidence of familiarity and out into a plaza.

Here the ashen floor was parted by a raised dais composed of gothic tortoiseshell. Atop this a monolith stood as sentinel, a twisted spiral that shifted as if fleeting shadows passed its surface. It turned without moving to watch me pass.

At the base of one of the black spires, an aperture presented itself. My feet faltered for the first time. Not out of hesitation, but of reverence. I stood on the threshold, staring into the abyss, listening to the dark invitation that sounded silently in my mind.

I saw clearly, even in the spire's pitch interior. I expected nothing so uniform as stairs, but a slope led upwards around the non-circular spire's inner wall. The worn soles of my old trainers sought for purchase and failed, sliding on the pock-marked surface and I had to lay my hands on the slick ground several times to keep my footing. I refused to let my hand stray to the wall for fear of what I would find there. So, it seemed there was still a heart of human emotion in me after all. Somehow, the revelation only made me feel more vulnerable.

On I climbed.

I passed archways, toppled or blocked, but didn't care for what they contained. No curiosity made me halt my upward progress. I knew they weren't the places for me.

The fifth floor was the worst.

Here the slope ended at the entrance to a narrow

corridor that spanned the abyss below. Despite the total darkness I could see that the slope continued at the furthest end. I would need to cross.

The walls pressed against me and at several points I had to squeeze between the walls sideways. This was when I felt the first warmth in this otherwise bleak place. There was no comfort in it as the walls emitted only a tepid temperature that drew further attention to the cold. Stopping dead in one of these tight spots, the damp lukewarmth licking at my crawling skin, I heard a faint sound. Like the slow click of a broken football rattle or the turning of an ancient portcullis far beneath the earth. The temperature increased slightly where my face nearly touched the uneven marble surface. I knew then that the warmth came not from the walls but from something beyond. Something that could hear me, as I had heard it, and that moved closer to examine me.

I admit that I ran, crabwise, shuffling in my haste to leave the claustrophobic space.

Don't look back, I thought. *For the love of God don't look back.*

I recited this like a mantra taught to me in my crib, and every time I uttered the name of God, I felt a knot of nausea inside.

Upwards, upwards. I found that I was becoming almost goatish in my surefootedness. The higher I climbed, the more my feet knew the way.

It was a long while before another archway approached. The distance between floors was becoming greater. The opening hung with curtains of glistening mould that swayed heavily in a putrid breeze. An air of ancient decay assaulted me; *eau de crypt,* the scent of choice. My stomach lurching, I didn't wait to see what might present itself from that archway. My imagination assaulted me with images I hoped were worse than anything that could realistically appear. And I knew I was wrong.

Finally I risked a rest on the cold, slick surface of the slope. Finding a place where the rivets and craters would accommodate my aching body took several moments. I hung my head between my knees and let the tiredness wash over me. Had I ever felt tired in a dream before? Had I ever ached? Had I ever been aware that I was dreaming? If you fell asleep in a dream, surely you would wake in the real world. I knew that if you died in your dreams the real body could not survive the death of the mind. That was surely why you still felt fear in dreams.

Before I could test my theories and drift into a vulnerable sleep, my heavy eyelids snapped open like those of a cornered rabbit. I sat shuddering with the effort of remaining still and silent, my breath held to burning point. A sound. Another sound. A gentle shushing that tormented harsh syllables from soft sounds. This voice was one I knew. This was the same seduction that had drawn me into the tower.

Closer now. Much closer.

The remainder of my ascent was made in a slippery scramble. I couldn't see, but could feel the grime that now covered my hands and I was sure that they bled. The darkness had become so thick that I could almost taste its tangy gloom on my tongue. I didn't know what I climbed toward, only that I had no choice in the matter. No, that isn't true. I had a choice, I just didn't want to stop. Nothing would have stopped me topping the slope's final rise to stand there panting and awestruck.

The space in which I now stood is hard to describe. I can see it in my mind's eye but words of adequate description fail me. All I'll say is that it was an amphitheatre of sorts, made of the same dark materials as the other structures I had seen. Hangings of grotesque gratuity hung on some walls, some of their designs gratefully obscured beyond comprehension by their shredded nature, the rest by grime.

Upon an ivory pillar that would make the Parthenon feel inadequate stood a throne. It wasn't made for human seating, that was certain. Its size alone told me that. It resembled a bowl; a high-backed bowl with its foremost edge turned down.

That sound. That dithering exhalation and its diabolical words so close that I could smell iron in the blood-tinged breath that uttered them.

Craning my neck upwards I saw its source hidden in the shadows. So magnificent was it that I couldn't even manage a gasp or exhalation. Struck dumb, I couldn't utter the shriek of dread that my mind wanted to. My knees locked, forbidding me from pressing myself to the ground in an effort to retreat as far from the hanging colossus as I could.

It seemed to taste my voiceless emotion, jittering with hunger or excitement. It moved, liquid in the dark. Not toward me, but toward the throne. Finally I closed my burning eyes so tight and simply stood listening to the sounds of its locomotion. Its bulk writhed along the amphitheatre's walls, grinding against stone, dislodging some. It became almost silent for a moment and I wondered if it had ceased to move. Maybe it hadn't noticed me before and now it had. Maybe it watched me with impossible eyes. I don't think I made a conscious decision to look, but my eyes opened when it uttered one of its whispers.

With words that I couldn't comprehend it seemed to say, *See me.*

I caught sight of things that my eyes denied. My brain tried foolishly and in vain to apply the laws of biology to what I saw in silhouette. That appeared to be a shoulder, that the dip of a hip or a hand. Such was my perception subject to change in the dark.

One thing was certain: the throne was made for

this creature, this Kraken or Dark God. It rested. One tendril flipped and twined lazily around the pillar's girth, the only part of this abstract that I could clearly see.

Was this the beast that had called me from so far away? Was I drawn to this fiend by its will or my own?

We watched each other, mutually rapt.

Had the infernal creature struck at me, lunged forward with its gaping maw and swallowed me whole or ground my bones to paste I wouldn't have been surprised. In fact, I was expecting nothing less.

But I woke.

Its final stammering whisper echoed in my ears as I searched my room in disbelief. Painful light stabbed at my crusted eyes from between the blinds. I felt like a prisoner who had clawed his way from an oubliette only to find that he could no longer stand the sun and must remain in the darkness. Realising that I wasn't breathing, I coughed violently and choked on my own lack of saliva. Rolling onto my side as the spluttering died away, I'm not ashamed to say that I held myself tightly for a long time and stared at the wall. If I closed my eyes I was certain that there would be no return for me. I still feel the same way.

Dreams are unbelievable by their very nature. They don't hold to laws of time or space and pay no heed to our human logic. That's why I know that what I had was no dream. It was fantastical, petrifying, and impossible. But as I searched my hands for grime and blood in the cold light of this morning, as I hunted hungrily for the trainers that I was convinced would retain some mark of the slate-coloured ash, I knew that my dream wasn't a dream.

It wasn't a dream.

Daisy Chained

DAISY JENKINS LIES on the floor of her bedroom. Her blonde hair, straight from the bottle, spills over a face that rests on folded hands. Sprawled across the floorboards, her legs twine around themselves. The dusk light, filtered through half-open blinds, bathes the room in ochre and twinkles from the handcuffs that attach her ankle to the radiator. She would appear to be asleep except for the quivering in her slender frame.

Until now, her day has been mundane…

SLAPPING THE ALARM clock as if it were carrying out some personal vendetta, Daisy allows herself a groan and five more minutes. She uses the time to ponder over who should occupy the empty space beside her.

Out of bed and into her robe.

Her morning ablutions she performs on auto-pilot, remaining half asleep even as she brushes her hair and flosses her teeth. Not until she shambles through the kitchen does she open her eyes. Swaying in front of the coffee percolator, Daisy perches tiptoe on the cold tiles. The coffee is bitter and adding milk does little for the taste, neither does sugar. She promises herself to maybe buy instant. Her face scrunches with each reluctant sip, but the murky liquid rouses her senses for the next delicate task.

Her make-up bag sits beside yesterday's paper, which she ignores, as she did yesterday. She pours out the contents of the small bag, but selects only mascara and foundation. Paying particular attention to a small blemish in her jaw line, an old scar, Daisy checks her mirror. She doesn't linger on the reflection.

A grid of November grins at her from the far wall. Crosses scar the grid, ending in a red circle. Daisy slashes it through, almost tearing the page, and turns away.

A knock at the door. Daisy checks the clock, and answers.

"Good morning, young lady. Did I wake you?"

The old guy from next door. She has no idea what his name is, but in her mind she calls him Frank.

"I was up."

"Slave to the corporate wage, eh?" He laughs at his own joke. "Can I interest you in-"

"No," says Daisy. "You can't. I am not, nor have I ever been interested."

"Well, there's no need to be like tha-"

"I've lived here for three months, and never, ever have I let you in, accepted your leaflets, or listened to your drivel. Jesus does *not* want me for a moonbeam. He is *not* on my Christmas list. The only Holy Spirit I ever come in contact with is a double of Russian Standard. Please leave me alone."

The door clicks in the jamb, leaving the neighbour to regard the woodwork.

Daisy bites on her lip, letting pain dull her anger. The circle on the calendar watches her from across the room.

She plucks her work clothes from the wardrobe door, trousers inside blouse inside jacket; shoes underneath.

The bedside clock gives her an hour before work.

FIRST SCUTTLING BACK into her flat for the folder that was impossible to forget, Daisy darts down the stairs cursing the second cup of coffee and Philip Schofield. From his doorway, the neighbour spies her leaving and creeps across the hall to slide his leaflet beneath the door. It reads: *Is your soul ready for heaven?*

Daisy dodges raindrops and puddles.

The commute is an easy one. The bus route takes

her into the town centre, a place built with a grey upon grey motif, and a brisk walk brings her to the door of her building. Despite the short journey she manages to be drenched by a passing taxi. She catches the full force on herself, protecting the folder under her arm. For the rest of the day her left shoe squelches; when she sits, the damp patch on the seat of her trousers soaks further. Daisy mutters threats to the folder until Damian finally arrives to claim it.

He slurs her name in country drawl. A childish taunt. Daisy is well aware that she probably shares her name with a battalion of Somerset cows and doesn't need anyone to remind her. She smiles politely as he patronises her.

"You know, Daisy, one day you might be in my position and you'll understand why I'm so hard on you. It's a lot more responsibility being supervisor, you see. It's my job to make sure you do your best-"

Daisy's heart races. She can feel her face tightening, drawing the smile into a grimace. Her jaw clenches until her gums ache with the pressure.

"-at the end of the day, I'm doing you a favour."

Damian stops. His brow furrows. He steps back. Snatching the folder, he retreats across the office, throwing backward glances. His door slams closed.

Daisy can taste blood.

She spins around, searching for the mirror in her handbag. She checks her mouth, wincing as her

68

finger probes the cut in her cheek. Her tongue feels rough, a little too big for her mouth. She stumbles from her cubicle, and gulps three cups of water from the cooler.

RAIN DRUMS THE window.

The coffee wore off an hour ago.

Daisy's eyes stray to the clock on her monitor.

AT FOUR-FIFTEEN, LOUISE'S head rises over the cubicle wall. At first Daisy makes excuses. She's tired, she doesn't feel well, Damian has broken her will to live. Louise only becomes more adamant.

Daisy spends their time in the café-bar checking her watch.

"I'll have a hot chocolate," says Louise.

"Would you like cream and a flake with that?" asks the waitress.

"Why not! I'll re-start the diet Monday."

"And for you?"

"Double vodka and coke. No ice," says Daisy.

The waitress scribbles, and leaves.

"Bloody hell, Daze. You starting early?"

"Something like that."

"You shouldn't let Damian get to you, you know. He's a prick. Not worth worrying about. You want something to eat?"

"No thanks," says Daisy. "I'll probably eat later.

Do you have the right time?"

"Am I boring you?" says Louise through a smile.

"Course not. I'm just tired. I should get an early night."

"Well just for the next half an hour, forget about everything, ok? Drink your dirty coke and relax. Consider this an intervention, Daze. We need to get you out. We need to get you a man. We need to get you a life!"

THE VODKA, AND the next, smoothes the edges of Daisy's nerves. Louise talks and Daisy listens. She even laughs. The bar fills with the post-work crowd, and empties again.

"…I swear, it was like a baby's arm holding a peach!" says Louise.

Daisy snorts, a little of the drink rising in her nose. She laughs until tears form in her eyes. Wiping them with a napkin, she spots the clock above the bar.

All the blood drains from her face.

She dives from her seat, knocking over a pile of plates from the bar as she stumbles. Cheap crockery shards explode across the floor.

"Daze, you ok?" says Louise.

Daisy makes a sound in her throat, but nothing that resembles a word.

"Daisy?" Louise starts to follow, but stops.

Daisy spins about, knocking the waitress from her high-heels with a yelp, and darts for the exit. The fascinated clientele begin to murmur; those in Daisy's way scrape their chairs and move aside.

Daisy hesitates at the door, and looks back. A crowd of curious, furious, and confused faces look back.

"I'm sorry," she mutters. "I'm sorry. Have to go."

The door slams.

PEOPLE WALK TOO slowly. Daisy drops from the curb and overtakes them, ignoring her sodden feet as she traipses through the gutter.

At the bus stop she jigs from foot to foot like an addict as the bus arrives late. Others in the queue give her a wide berth.

The bus gets stuck in traffic.

"Please, just let me off."

"I'm sorry, love. I can't. If you get run over, I'll never forgive myself."

Daisy's hand slams on the driver's booth; her breath fogs the glass in huffs. The driver slips back in his seat, despite the barrier. Daisy says something the other passengers don't hear, and the bus door clacks open.

Daisy leaps out, and sprints away.

DESPITE HER ADRENALIN, the run has made Daisy sluggish.

The climb to her floor seems like a mountain.

Her door sticks in the jamb.

Panting, sweat coursing down her neck, Daisy is in.

She kicks the leaflet aside, letting a snarl escape her throat.

The second hand makes easy work of the clock face.

Daisy kicks off her shoes. One lands in the living room, the other in the hall, dripping water and mud. Her jacket and trousers she throws through the bathroom door, and snatches a towel. The clock sounds its second alarm of the day as she fumbles in the drawer. With handcuffs in hand, Daisy sits by the radiator. It's an old, wrought iron affair. Brackets like girders and god-knows-how-many years of paint have set it like cement to the wall. Daisy rests her burning face against the cold metal.

Placing the tiny keys on the window ledge above her, Daisy is confident that she won't be able to use them until morning. She slips her ankle into one ring, wincing with each tightening click.

With quivering fingers she manages to unbutton her blouse. She tosses it as far across the room as she can. It lands on the far edge of the bed.

She sits for a while; allows her heart to slow, her

head to loll. Beads of perspiration line her neck and shoulders. With arms wrapped around her knees, she releases a long, shuddering breath.

THE DOOR BANGS.

Again.

The sound echoes around Daisy's flat.

Down the hall and through the door, the landlady's voice carries.

"Are you in, love?"

If I was in, I'd have answered.

"Daisy? Are you in?"

Obviously not. Now go away.

The sound of hefty shoes withers to silence.

Daisy lays herself down.

She thinks of anything except the failing light. She thinks about the folder at first, the proposal, and what Damian will say tomorrow. She thinks about Louise and what to tell her tomorrow. She thinks about tomorrow as if tonight doesn't exist.

She thinks about the cruelty of moonlight.

Her family. Daisy thinks about her family. Her mother and those who care for her, a father long gone. She tries to remember his face but the details are slipping. Her brother, and if he'll come home safe. October is so far away.

As dusk fades to night, Daisy can think of nothing but the darkness. The Moon rises somewhere beyond the windowsill. She watches stripes of silver light creep across her room; first over the bedcovers, then across the wall in slanted hound's teeth.

The Moon sings to Daisy.

She buries her head in her arms and shivers violently.

Prayers for a swift dawn.

A strangled whimper.

Tonight, the Moon will take her.

Tonight, Daisy must be chained.

Lindsay's Pride

L AUGHTER RIPPLED BELOW, almost loud enough for Lindsay to feel it through the floorboards. Mark's voice rumbled on for a minute and there was another peal of laughter; so many mouths and teeth and thrashing tongues.

If they'd have cared that she 'wasn't feeling well', they'd have kept the noise down. Or maybe even gone home so she and Mark could have the argument they needed. But they stayed, and that laughter would be at her expense. Mark would put his hand on his hip, waggle a finger on the other, and make his voice shrieking to imitate her. And *her* laughter would be loudest of all.

Sat on the edge of her bed, Lindsay's fingers twisted the duvet as if she had to hold on or fall. Her hair swayed with each sob, tickling her face. She brushed it back with one hand and lifted her chin. A sniff cleared her nose. She took a deep breath and released it fast. Rubbing her eyes only made the sting worse.

More laughter, rising from the space where Lindsay's toes curled into the carpet.

Adding insult to injury was the purpose of the party. Not Mark's birthday at all, but an exhibit; a parade of Lindsay in all her stupidity.

Inviting people from work was fine, Lindsay looked forward to playing wife and hostess for the evening. But inviting *her* was a slap in the face. When he talked to *her*, it was a kick in the guts. When he filled *her* glass it was a knife blade between the ribs.

Lindsay knew all about it. And everyone downstairs knew, too. And Mark, of course, knew it all. He just didn't care.

Standing, Lindsay's hand lashed out and grabbed the headboard. Her knees vibrated like tuning forks. Hand trailing the wall, she made her way to the bathroom, first stopping at the bedroom door.

It had gone awfully quiet downstairs.

Maybe they'd finally taken the hint.

The front door creaked, and the sound of quiet chatter drifted upstairs. Mark shouted a goodbye, a car door slammed. This happened a few times, at irregular intervals, volume dependent on the distance of the car.

The front door clicked closed.

He'd be up soon. Lindsay had to clean herself up. If they were going to argue, she couldn't look like she'd already been crying.

The bathroom light clicked twice before lighting, showing just how bad the damage was. Lindsay looked hideous. An oil pipeline had burst under each reddened eye, sending rivers of ink down her face. Her crows feet, just starting to show at the tender age of thirty-seven, were filled with liquid mascara, making them deep and ugly.

Lindsay turned this way and that, flattening her dress, cinching her waist with her hands. At a little over eleven stone, she was disgusting. There was little wonder Mark had strayed with *her*.

Her face never looked like that. *Her* arse was like a drum. *Her* stomach didn't need special pants to keep it in.

And those breasts.

Mark always said he loved Lindsay's breasts. He said it the first time they slept together and every time since. She'd been so embarrassed that she'd left her bra on. He'd been tender, asking her to remove it, and he'd kissed her there, telling her she was beautiful all the time. Lindsay melted from his flaming lies like candle wax and solidified at his feet, never to question him again. Until it was too late. And now he wanted breasts like *hers*. Like supermarket fruit.

The images were the worst. Of course he'd given no specifics, not even when she threw the plate at him and demanded to know. Not even when she hit him and he had to hold her down while she cried herself tired like a child. He just stood and denied everything. But Lindsay's imagination filled in the blanks.

Sat in front of the mirror, the cool flannel felt sensual on her face. But with her eyes closed, all the imaginings came back again. How his tongue would look, caressing *her* nipples as he did with Lindsay's. How his hands spread on the small of *her* back. How he would tilt his face into *her* neck and whisper old promises made new.

Lindsay retched, bringing wine-tinged bile into the bowl. Oh god, now she'd have to clean her teeth too. The wine (white was always a mistake) made her clumsy. The process was taking too long. But not as long as Mark was taking downstairs. He should have been up by now. It didn't take this long to lock up and turn out the lights. Or maybe he was hoping Lindsay would fall asleep so they didn't have to argue.

She carried on cleaning and drying, reapplying a little, finger-combing her hair. The dress would have to be changed. There was no way she felt good enough in it. Jeans would be better; the high-waisted ones. She'd had them years and could still fit into them. They made her feel good. Young again. Rash and powerful, even though she'd never been those things in her younger years.

A simple strappy top went with the jeans. No bra underneath. She wanted him to want her as she kicked him out of the door, to make him feel it in the only place he felt anything. Mark always told her how sexy she looked like this. And she'd caught him giving her that look too many times to think it another lie.

He gave *her* that look. When she leant over his desk. When the copier wouldn't work. When she brought him coffee and a come-on.

Just on the edge of hearing, the front door creaked again.

A moment.

Clicked shut; too quiet to be anything other than caution.

Fifteen minutes. Fifteen minutes after everyone else had left. While Lindsay was right upstairs. Waiting for him. Crying over him—

Lindsey stared at the bedroom door, her jaw slack. Her knees finally gave way and the bed caught her. Searching her palms for answers, she shook her head when none were found.

Mark's footsteps on the stairs.

Lindsey was up, and bolting for the bathroom. Make-up was scraped into the drawer under the sink.

The sink itself rinsed clean. There wasn't time to clear anything else.

When he came in, she was sat in front of the mirror but not looking into it.

Mark stood at the door for a while, watching her. She glanced up at his reflection. The bottom button of his shirt was undone, protruding from the waistband like a flag. There was something wet around the fly of his trousers, a darker patch of black as if he'd spilled his drink.

He stood with hands on hips; stretched his back. Satisfied.

Stepping into the bathroom, Lindsay could see his smirk; a glow in his cheeks.

He stepped up behind her, close enough to touch his crotch between her shoulder blades.

The scent of beer leaked off him. Beer, and a waft of alien perfume.

"What're you crying for, now?"

The hair dryer contacted Mark's temple so fast that he didn't blink. There was a flash of light as the fuses exploded. His legs collapsed. A dull crack echoed in the toilet as his forehead hit the lip of the bowl, and bounced off.

Lindsay opened her eyes.

The bathroom was dark.

A wedge of light from the bedroom lit Mark's twisted legs. The smell of burning came from the socket behind her. Pain in her fingers reminded her of the hair dryer. She let the plastic shell splinter on the tiles and watched as her knuckles turned pink. Her fingers shook, stomach churning like kneaded dough.

Something oozed around her bare foot, but was too far away for her to register.

All she saw was Mark's sock, worn bare at the heel, and twitching.

LINDSAY SEEMED NICE, if not a little quiet. And maybe a little spoilt. But that was only a first impression and Natalie didn't take as much stock in them as other people. When Lindsay had gone upstairs, Nat couldn't help noticing the sour look the hostess gave her. But it was neither woman's fault. Nat would have done the same thing if her husband had spent all night flirting with his assistant.

He spoke to other people, for the look of the thing, but every time Nat glanced his way Mark was already looking at her. She tried to talk to Lindsay a few times before she left; thank her for a lovely night and compliment the cheesecake (she had a weakness for it), but Lindsay made some excuse or moved away like a herded sheep. Mostly she disappeared into the kitchen, and Nat wasn't brave enough to follow.

Poor Lindsay. What must it be like to watch

your husband drool over a younger woman? Nat found it happened a lot. She was attractive, from a man's point of view, she had to admit. There was a wolf-whistle or chat up line waiting for her almost everywhere she went. And it was horrible.

When her friends dressed up, Nat dressed down. She'd spent her university years in baggy jumpers and jogging pants just to hide the figure beneath, hoping that a man would fall in love with her for her conversation or sense of humour. But they never did. Nat got the pricks and the egotists. The ones that thought good breeding was found through breast-shaped binoculars. But the older men were the worst.

It was obvious that Mark liked younger women. Lindsay must have been ten years his junior, and he married her; Nat was almost twenty years younger still, and so he wanted to shag her. Christ, he spent most of the work day drooling and dry-humping her desk. And if it wasn't for the fact that the job was perfect, and well paid, and that Nat knew her next boss would only be the same, she'd leave.

It was tiring.

Standing in front of the mirror in her living room, Nat turned this way and that.

She wished she saw what *they* did. But she just saw hips that bounced when she walked, breasts that hurt in the gym despite a sports bra made by the same people who designed the Humber Bridge. And she hated her feet (when she eventually caught sight of them, which wasn't often with those goddamn breasts in the way). Open-toed sandals and flip-flops were a no-go.

Lindsay's figure was perfect. The kind that could wear anything and not look slutty. The dress she'd had on tonight had been beautiful, the low back looking perfect on her petite frame. Nat would have looked like a slut in it. She looked like a slut in most things. And that's why her dress was high necked and cut to the knee. But the black material still made her breasts look like an approaching battleship, even with a full bodice strapped tight underneath.

It was no good. It had to come off.

Nat set her wine glass down on the mantelpiece and went upstairs.

It took two seconds to get out of the dress, but almost fifteen minutes to get out of the bodice.

If Mark had his way tonight, this would be the second time she'd removed it. The slimy bastard. While she had been in the toilet (desperately trying to wee despite the fact the bodice stopped her sitting down) he called it a night and everyone left. When she came back into the living room, Mark was sat in the chair, looking at her, waiting for her. Wearing that stupid "Birthday Boy" badge.

"Everyone's gone home," he said.

Nat panicked. She was acutely aware that Mark

was between her and the door. At least Lindsay was upstairs. Surely he wouldn't try anything now.

"I should be going too. Lots to do tomorrow," she said, and moved toward the door.

Mark stood.

"Am I giving you too much to do?"

"Not at all. It's good to be kept busy."

He was at the living room door, hand on the knob as if ready to open it, but not moving.

"I could reduce your work load to doing only *one* thing for me," he said, ignoring her response for the sake of a good come-on. He moved toward her, making her legs bump the sofa arm as she retreated. She almost fell.

He caught her. Stinking of that horrible cologne, he pulled her close to him.

"Woops. Had a little too much to drink, have we?"

His breath was all over her face, stinking of beer and the chili he'd wolfed down.

She turned away, forcing her hands into his chest.

"Not *that* much, Mark."

He stopped for a moment when his enthusiasm wasn't returned, just long enough for Nat to prize herself away and move back across the room.

"Oh," he said. His face caved in, leaving only an old man's leer sipping from his pint glass. He perched on the sofa's arm, stroking the place where Nat's bum had contacted it.

She shivered despite the warm summer night.

"I should really go." She didn't move. She'd still have to squeeze past him to get to the door if she tried to leave now.

"Shall I call you a cab?"

"No. Thank you. I can be home by the time it arrives."

"A woman like you shouldn't be walking around at night on her own."

I'm more worried about being in here *on my own,* she thought. *Mugging might be a welcome alternative.*

"I'll be fine. I know how to kick where it hurts."

"Yes. I'm sure you know *exactly* where that is."

And that was it. He was drunk. She would never be drunk enough. What was a stupid man flirting with a young woman had turned into a pathetic old creep sexually harassing her.

"Mark," she said. "I'm leaving. Now. Please move away from the door."

He *humph*ed like a child and swung his leg over the sofa's arm, sliding down onto it. He was trying to look cool and nonchalant, but spilt his drink in the meantime.

"Bollocks," he said as Nat bolted for the door. He grabbed at his shirt, dabbing it against his trousers, only dampening both garments more.

She found the front door unlocked and moved out onto the doorstep.

Mark's hand wrapped around her wrist. Pain sparkled for a moment, so she didn't resist when he span her toward him. He was even closer this time. Close enough for her to feel what was barely a bump beneath his trousers. He worked it into her thigh for a moment, expecting her to warm to the idea.

Nat had had enough.

There was pushing it and then too far. This was beyond either.

She jerked her knee enough to startle him, but not do any permanent damage.

He let go pretty quickly.

She bolted down the path, letting the gate collide with the garden wall, and out into the street. She might have heard the door close.

Finally back in the safety of her own bedroom, she'd worked the bodice loose and took a few deep breaths as it creaked off.

Thank god.

The night had been full of discomfort and upset. All she wanted was to crawl into her pyjamas, finish her wine, and go to bed.

A knock at the door.

Hurrying into her pyjamas, and throwing the flannel dressing gown over, Nat wondered who the hell could be knocking.

As she reached the staircase, she thought of Mark. Would he be drunk enough, stupid enough, to follow her home. If it was him, the police would find out which.

Taking all possible care, Nat teased the living room curtain away from the wall and peered through. It was dark, and she could barely see. But it definitely wasn't Mark.

It looked like—

No.

Why would she come here?

What had Mark said to her? What had his stupid pride and throbbing trouser-ego made him say?

LINDSAY LOOKED TERRIBLE.

She'd been crying. Even with the new make-up, Nat could see the swollen eyes.

"Can I come in?"

"It's kind of late," said Nat. "Can it wait?"

"No."

"Oh."

Nat moved aside and Lindsay let herself in.

"Lindsay, listen, I don't know you and you really don't know me. But I'm just going to say this and have done with it. Because I think your being here is due to a major misunderstanding. Or maybe lies. Either way, I want you to know that your husband is a bastard. He's a letch and that's all he is. I wouldn't touch him with a barge-pole. Not that I'm saying he's unattractive. You know, he's your husband and I'm sure you love him, but he's definitely not my type and *definitely* not in my age range. He's flirted with me ever since I started at Harker's, and apparently he did it with the girl before too. He just can't keep it to himself. It's not my fault, and I never gave him any idea that I was interested-"

Lindsay just stood in front of the gas fire, staring at a patch of wall a foot behind Nat's chest.

"Lindsay?"

Nothing.

"Lindsey? Are you alright? What's he done? You can tell me."

"Do you have any more of that?" Lindsay raised a finger to the wine glass on the mantelpiece.

"Yeah. Yes, of course."

Nat disappeared into the kitchen and poured a glass of red. She brought the bottle in with her. This was going to be a long night.

Lindsay still stood where Nat had left her.

"Why don't you sit down?"

Lindsay obeyed and took the wine glass when it was offered.

"Do you want to tell me what he's done?"

"He's a bastard," said Lindsay.

"Yes, he is."

"He has affairs. He's done it before."

"I'm so sorry, Lindsay."

"I thought he was doing it with you, too."

"I swear to you, he hasn't. Not with me."

"But he's done it before."

"Yes, I guess he has."

"What happened to your wrist?"

She'd been rubbing it without noticing. There were deep purple marks growing through the skin. Four in a row. Four little piggys.

"Nothing."

"He grabbed you didn't he? He likes grabbing. It hurts." Lindsay's eyes burnt into the stripes on Nat's wrist.

"Yes. He did. But it doesn't hurt much. It's just a little sore. Nothing a few bangles won't cover up."

Lindsay hung her head, arms resting on knees, wine glass held in both hands like a sacrificial offering of blood.

"I think I killed him."

"I'm sorry?"

"I'm sure I killed him. His foot…and the blood…"

Nat finally noticed what she should have long before.

"I thought…I thought he'd done it again…"

Lindsay's bare feet were stained red with congealed blood.

"I couldn't stand it…you're so pretty…he likes

you…"

Some had flaked off as she walked into the living room, and again when she moved to the sofa.

"He looks at you…but what you said…and he hurt you…"

Mark's drying blood was on Nat's floor.

Ohmygod. Ohmygod. Ohmygod.

Lindsay was looking at her. Her eyebrows were high, a weak smile on her lips. Tears streaked her face.

"I did it for both of us."

Nat couldn't look up. Her wine glass hung slack in her fingers.

"Can I use your bathroom?" asked Lindsay.

Nat heard it as if through a curtain of panic. "What?"

"Your bathroom. Can I use it?"

Nat just looked at her; nodded.

Lindsay got up, taking her wine with her, and made for the stairs.

"Natalie," she said. "I'm sorry. Tell them I'm sorry."

"Who?" asked Nat.

Lindsey just smiled, and headed for the stairs.

Nat listened to the stranger's footsteps creak up the narrow stairs, shuffling across the carpet above, and the bathroom door clicked shut. She moved like lightning, setting the wine down on the table, grabbing for the phone, jabbing the number on reflex.

She whispered fast and quiet, eyes fixed on the living room door.

"Police, police…hello? Hello? Hi. My name's Natalie Brewster. I'm at 1-9-2 Rowan Court. I need a policeman. Now. There's a woman in my house and she says she killed her husband. I work for her husband, you see, but she's in my house and she's covered in his blood. She's in my bathroom. She wanted to use the bathroom. I need a policeman. Please. Send someone-"

The sound of smashing glass from above.

"Ohmygod, ohmygod. She just broke something up there. Please, send someone. Please."

NAT STOOD ON the opposite curb, pulses of blue light splashing her face. Someone had given her a blanket. She couldn't remember who.

Three police cars parked at odd angles to her house. Two more cordoned off either end of the street. Neighbours she'd never seen before crowded any pavement the police would let them. Radios crackled and squeaked.

Paramedics rattled the trolley over the front step and slid it into the ambulance. Muttering rose from the crowd. The form beneath the cover had been too obvious even to them.

A young policeman was gently probing her for answers.

"Miss Brewster?" his pen wavered over a blank page. "Did she say anything?"

"No," said Nat. "I mean, yes. She said she'd killed him, and…she was sorry."

Nat burst into tears. The officer caught her as her knees buckled, and sat with her on the pavement while she shook and sobbed.

The ambulance drew away, not bothering to use the siren.

Sarah and the Monster

1

Leave the door open, Mummy."

This was the routine.

If truth be told, Jennifer liked the door open as much as Sarah did. There had never been a time in all the seven years of her daughter's life when Jennifer had been able to shake the sensation of imminent danger to her child. Her own mother said Jennifer was overcautious, that she never mollycoddled *her* as a child; her husband said she was wrapping Sarah in cotton wool and that the girl would never grow up if Jennifer didn't let her. Jennifer secretly ignored any of his comments, he wasn't the girl's father and so would never truly understand.

"Goodnight, sweetie. Sleep tight." Blowing a kiss, Jennifer stayed to make sure her daughter snuggled down under the covers.

WITH HER MOTHER finally gone, Sarah peeked back out of the covers. The door was still a little too closed for her liking, and so she quickly slid out of bed to widen the gap. Safely back beneath the heavy down quilt, Sarah fumbled for the torch beneath her pillow. There was still time for more reading before she would be tired, and beneath the covers was the perfect place to do it.

Sarah was top of her class for reading. In fact, she was top of the class above too. She held the shrewd curiosity of a seven-year old that was going on seventy in the head, and read books like most people breathe. Crisp, the pages *whipp*ed as they turned. Sarah's teacher thought the loud page turning to be a sign of showing off. Sarah simply liked the draught; the way it carried a scent of the page; how her hair fluttered and tickled her cheek just above the dimple.

"*Sarah? Sarah, are you asleep?*"

She paused mid-turn.

That wasn't her mother.

It wasn't her stepfather.

"*Sarah, I know you're awake, I can hear you hold-ing your breath. I won't hurt you, come out.*" That voice, like broken glass in honey.

Slowly, she peeped above the flowery geography of her duvet.

Nothing. No one.

The open door cast a wedge of light across the

foot of her bed. This time, she didn't imagine desert where the hills and valleys of light cast dune-like shadows; she was a little preoccupied. Moving to speak, or rather to call for her mother, she found that the fear goblin had stolen her voice. He had stuffed it into his pointy hat made of clogged rat fur and ran off with it, cart wheeling and japing as he went.

"*That's better. I hate talking to myself,*" continued the voice.

"W-where are you?" asked Sarah.

"*I'm sorry?*" The voice sounded startled. It certainly startled Sarah. "*Don't you want to know who I am?*"

"No. I want to know *where* you are. I want to know where you are so that you can not be there anymore, please," said Sarah with the determination of a little woman.

Sarah searched the floor, as far into the hallway as she could see, behind the curtains, while staying firmly in bed. The initial fear had sunk somewhat, shoved aside by her curiosity.

There was a silence for a moment, then a chuckle like the sound of loose teeth in a bag.

"*Clever girl. I'm behind the door.*"

"You can't be. There's no room."

"*I'll admit it's a little cosy.*"

"I mean there's no room for a full person back there. You're lying."

"*Sarah, I want us to be friends, and so I'll only say this once.*" Calm as custard, the voice lowered to a menacing crackle. "*Never call me a liar again.*"

Sinking back into her pillows, shielding herself with the covers, Sarah was certain that she had felt a foul breath touch her face; a breath that harboured the smell of fresh tar and eggs. There was a malice hidden below its surface, like a bloated corpse under thin ice.

"*Now we know each other a little-*" the voice said, sedate once more. "*Sarah. Sarah come out from under there….good girl. I do so hate being ignored. Now we know each other a little better, I came here to tell you that something is coming for you. Not tonight, but soon, and you don't want what will happen to happen. I'm here to help.*"

"What do you want?" managed Sarah.

"*I just told you,*" said the voice. "*I want to help.*"

"I want you to go away," said Sarah, quietly.

"*No you don-*"

"Go away."

"*Sara-*"

"Go *away.*"

Castles of comfort rising on either side of her, Sarah burrowed; misty eyes fixed on the open door. She stared until her eyes ached.

Slowly but surely, her blinks became slower; eyes staying shut for longer and longer until they didn't open at all.

2

"MUMMY, CAN YOU close the door?"

Jennifer stopped dead in the doorway. Seeing the surprise on her mother's face, Sarah tried to explain. "I'm a big girl now, and big girls don't leave their door open."

"Yes, that's right," said Jennifer through the shock. "I'm right down the hall if you need me. Sweet dreams, sweetie."

Unable to bring herself to close the door fully, Jennifer left a slight gap. The longer that door stayed open, the longer Sarah would be her little girl. From here on it would be closed bedroom doors, then secret diaries, then boys. Maybe she was overreacting a little, but Jennifer couldn't help feeling that this small step was the beginning of the end for Sarah's innocence.

SARAH DELVED DEEP into her nightly womb. She had spoken to her friend, Lily, about the Bogeyman. Sarah had never been afraid of anything sinister in the dark, but now she had good reason. Lily's parents said the Bogeyman didn't exist, but Lily didn't believe them. If she was scared Sarah should hide under the covers; it was a well-known fact that he couldn't get you under your covers.

Curled tight as a hamster, Sarah tried not to think about the voice from the night before. Still, as she drifted off to sleep, the heat from her breath making an oven of her den, dark images began to form in her mind, stoking the brimstone furnace where nightmares are made.

"-rah. Sarah, wake up."

Not you again.

"Sarah, listen to me. Come out."

"No," said Sarah, her voice muffled by the duvet. "You just want me to come out so you can get me. Lily says you can't get me as long as I'm in here."

"Lily's an idiot," said the voice. "If I wanted to eat you, you'd be turning on a spit with a an apple in your broken teeth. But I've eaten, that's why I'm late."

Against her better judgement, she risked a peek. The voice wasn't where it had been the night before. It had a stifled sound, as if contained....he was in the toy box. Breaking her things as he sat his slimy, hairy body on them; playing with her dolls in the dark. It was almost too much for her to stand.

"What do you want? Leave me alone," whimpered Sarah, her eyes trained on the toy box's lid, slightly ajar. There were too many toys in there and the lid had never closed. Was there a movement in the darkness? As if something shifted its weight?

"There's a Monster coming for you, Sarah. Not tonight, but soon. It's coming for you and I don't want it *to get you.*"

"The only monster is you," said Sarah, tired and deathly afraid.

"*I'm a different type of monster.*"

"All monsters are the same. Go away," Sarah said, with tears in her voice.

He was gone.

3

"Mummy?"

"Yes, sweetie?"

"I love you."

"I love you too, Darling." Jennifer came back into the room and sat on Sarah's bed. "Where did that come from?"

"I just wanted you to know, that's all."

Sarah had been quiet. Eating her breakfast, Jennifer had pestered. Sarah had been having nightmares. In a way, she was proud of her little girl for not calling for her in the night; in another, she hated not being there.

"Shall I leave the door open tonight?"

"No. It won't make any difference," said Sarah. "I'll try to sleep. Is it ok to read a little first?"

"Of course. But don't stay up too late."

"I won't."

"Sweet dreams."

THIS TIME SHE would be ready.

Sarah sat enveloped in her pillows; the furry pink one, the one embroidered with birds, the white one, almost as big as her, that she liked to lay on the floor with. A book propped open on her lap for the look of the thing, she searched the room. Her door was closed, the toy box was propped open with a small umbrella. She had no doubt in her mind that he would come again, but she wasn't going to make it easy for him.

The hour rolled out; not a single page of her book was turned.

SARAH WOKE WITH a start, her eyes snapping open. There was silence in the room, but she could feel the same foul breath she had felt before. It carried images with it; dark hallucinations of things little girls shouldn't consider.

He was close. He was watching her.

"I know you're here," she said.

No answer.

"Where are you?"

Nothing.

Anticipation of his sweet crackled voice was worse than actually hearing it. Sarah wanted to hear him. She wanted to know once and for all why he visited her, what he wanted, and to send him away forever.

"Talk to me. Where are you? What do you want?"

"Oh, you want to talk to me now do you?"

Sarah physically jumped, her book sliding off the bed and onto the floor. His voice was so close. She tucked her knees up under her chin, buried her face. This was it. The other nights were appetisers. Tonight was the night she would be taken.

"Oooh, The Worst Witch. Never seen that *one before."*

"You're….under my bed?" Sarah could feel her face tightening, as it did before the tears came. Her eyes stung, her chest felt like that of a small bird. Still, she leaned slightly, not wanting to see but needing to.

"Bingo," said the voice. *"This is your last chance, Sarah. The Monster is coming for you tonight. He's close. Real close. If you don't leave with me, you'll regret it. I can take you away, you'll be safe, but you have to hurry."*

There was an urgency, a pleading to the voice that Sarah hadn't expected. It sounded like Mummy telling her to be careful playing in the street.

From outside the door came a creak of floorboard.

"It's coming."

Sarah regarded the door with astonishment. The voice hadn't been lying.

"What is it?" asked Sarah, her surprise temporarily overtaking her fear.

"*A very bad Thing.*"

"How bad?"

"*There's still time. Get under the bed, Sarah. Quickly. I'll take you away. Get under th-*"

The thin beam of hallway light spread across Sarah's bed; the search light of the hungry Monster. Sarah hunkered down, intending to hide beneath the covers, but couldn't move.

"Voice," she whispered, her own full of tremor. "Voice, help me."

There was no answer. The voice was gone.

Sarah's chest began to spasm with silent sobs. The tears wouldn't come. Even her body had abandoned her.

The Monster stood in her open doorway, silhouetted by the hallway light.

It stood there, watching her for a moment. Stepping across the threshold, it spoke:

"Sarah? You ok, sweetie? I heard you talking."

Sarah wiped her stinging eyes.

Jennifer sat on the bed, letting her daughter fold into her lap. Sarah wiped tears onto her pyjama sleeve as Jennifer stroked her hair.

"It was just a bad dream, sweetie."

Sarah said nothing.

"It's over now. Why don't you try to sleep, and

I'll leave the door open when I go, eh?"

"It's ok Mummy, you go back to sleep. I don't think It'll be coming back."

"Well, if you're sure. But call if you need me ok?"

Jennifer climbed off the bed and almost fell.

"Ouch!"

"Mummy!?"

Sarah darted to the edge of the bed just in time to see some dark shape flicker beneath.

"Ouch!" repeated Jennifer. "What the hell did I stand on?"

"Mummy, get on the bed!"

"It's ok, Honey. Probably just one of your toys. Sweet dreams."

She kissed Sarah's head and limped out into the hallway light.

Waiting for the sound of Jennifer's bedroom door, she spoke:

"You're still here."

Silence.

You better believe it.

"What do you want?"

You're a sharp kid, Sarah. Figure it out.

Sarah tucked her feet up under the duvet, pulling it to her chest. If he came for her, she'd hide.

"You want to eat me?" she said. Her dry throat made her voice hoarse. She could feel it tightening as her breathing quickened.

Not right away.

"What *are* you?" she whimpered.

Hungry.

A scrape from one of the room's shadows made her dive under her covers.

The sound of wood scraping on wood.

The chair. The chair in the corner. He was sat right there, if only she was brave enough to look.

In the sanctuary of her duvet, everything had gone quiet. Her breathing was ragged but she couldn't hear it for the pounding of blood in her ears. She squeezed her eyes shut and prayed for morning. What time was it? Was it soon?

Air exploded around Sarah as her duvet was torn away. It flew up toward the ceiling and away as if let loose on the wind. Sarah tried to scream but her throat was tight. She rolled, scrambled and fought across the bed, leaping onto the floor. Running for the corner, she span around.

The room was perfectly still; perfectly dark but for the sliver of hallway light. Her duvet lay across the room in a crumpled heap. Something rustled the material around like a dog getting comfortable.

Sarah bunched her shoulders, trying to get closer to the wall. Through the crack in the door, the hallway light fell across her bed, cutting the room in two and coming to rest in the corner she stood in.

Sarah curled her toes into the carpet, moving herself back into the light.

Something shifted in the dark.

That breath again. The scent of boiling earth.

You can't hide forever, Sarah. Sometime you'll fall asleep. Then I'll have you. I may be hungry, but I can wait.

Sarah fought for breath.

The darkness stirred as if it were tar that the voice's owner moved through, seeming to give way for his invisible mass.

Or maybe I don't have to wait.

Sarah held her breath. She wanted so badly to cry, to scream, for the door to be thrown open and her Mummy to come in.

After all, I'm a connoisseur. Little girl isn't the only thing on the menu. There are other treats in this house.

Sarah looked out into the darkness.

"Puh-please…" She almost stepped forward but stopped herself.

Sarah started to weep.

Oh, give up. I'm losing my patience with you, Sarah. You were so fun at first. I think you need to decide, and quickly. Or I'll eat your Mummy and come back for you tomorrow. I don't normally double-dip. But for you I'll make an exception.

Sarah wept and wept, dropping to her knees in the band of light.

The darkness listened for a while.

That's enough. I'm not waiting anymore.

"No!" Sarah yelled. "Please! Not Mummy!"

Then who?

"Jack."

Who?

"Jack," said Sarah. "Take Jack instead."

That sounds like a dog's name to me. You trying to buy me off with a mutt? The voice turned to a hiss that made Sarah shiver. The darkness pressed tight around her. *You know how insulting that is?*

"He's with Mummy, next door."

Oh, Sarah, that's so low. That laugh again. *I love it.*

Jennifer burst into the door, throwing it wide and scattering the shadows.

"Baby? What are you doing down there?"

She darted over, wrapping herself around Sarah's shivering frame. They rocked together, Jennifer making soft sounds while her daughter sobbed.

"What's that, Honey? Did you say something?"

"I'm sorry, Mummy," said Sarah. "I'm so sorry."

Through the wall, they heard the first of Jack's screams.

Albert

1

'D QUICKLY LEARNT not to chase his mind, instead waiting for it to loop back around to reality. He mumbled and gesticulated, sometimes wildly as if conducting an orchestra, sometimes wistfully, tired.

There was a howl of human anguish in an adjoining room. Feet passed the door in a hurry. Albert didn't seem to register the sounds. Against green linoleum and whitewash he sat like an eerie exhibit; head in knees, hairy toes and forearms exposed. A white bracelet displayed his name and a barcode. The movements of his breathing could have been a trick of the eye.

The scream beyond the wall reached its height, was joined by muffled grunts of the staff, and then died away as if the patient were falling into the distance.

The silence allowed me to continue.

"Are you alright, Albert?" I asked in my best calming voice. The smell of pine-smothered urine dried my mouth. "Do you want a drink of water?"

Albert recoiled, knocking the glass from my hand with a flailing foot. To the sound of shattering glass, he scampered away. With his head buried in the corner, only a roll of humped shoulder and one pale foot were on show.

Rubbing at my stunned fingers, I understood why I was here.

Ringed eyes gave him the look of a petrified raccoon; he winced when his dry lips smacked together. Beneath the thin standard-issue pyjamas his chest expanded like a bird cage beneath a tarpaulin.

Somewhere along some distant corridor the cleaner's buffer whirred. I blotted my damp sleeve against my jeans.

I had little time here. The orderlies would come soon, all sweat and brute force. They would restrain him, tranquilise him if need be, and try to pump fluid into his tired veins. I could already see bruises where the needle had been, spreading like shadows beneath his skin. This man's delusions were killing him. Sitting in the Asylum's therapy room, I was certain that they already had.

His hydrophobia was an extension of some delusion. That was simple. How that delusion fit with the Cormouth case was beyond me. The police called for me infrequently; this time to speak with their only witness. But it wasn't my job to understand the larger picture.

I could still feel where the pillow had ruffled my hair to a cowlick. Waiting for Albert's next contribution, I absently tried to stroke it flat. I had a feeling that it would be morning before I was reacquainted with my bed. The thought of it growing cold without me seemed horrible.

"I'm sorry, Albert," I said. "Are you alright to talk?"

"Talk, no. I don't need to talk," he said, his voice muffled by the whitewashed surface he pressed himself against.

That was progress, a brief moment of lucidity. The first I'd seen.

"If we don't talk, how can I help you?"

"I already know," he rasped.

I made a note of that on my pad.

What does he know? Could I have found an opening so early on?

Following the thoughts of a mad man can be straining for the sane. Constantly fighting against our predisposition to logic; trying to make sense of the nonsensical. Over the years my frustration had gotten the better of me. In years gone-by, I would have been taking a break before my own sanity went the way of the dodo. But I wasn't ready for that yet.

Experience had taught me to enjoy this verbal jousting.

"Shouldn't you tell me then? So that I can know too?"

"No. No, I won't. I wa' worthy. He didn't take me. I 'ad to figure it out for myself. You should too," he said, and fell silent.

Outside, thunderclouds skidded across the sky, the colour of Albert's bruises. I understood that he must be restrained for his own good, to keep him alive. I understood that his old frame would mark easily with so little water in it. Still, some of the bruises were obviously finger-shaped. I cringed.

"Albert?" It had been a long while since he'd spoken, or moved. I felt my time running short. I repeated, without allowing urgency to enter my voice, "Albert?"

He made a small sound of confirmation but stayed still.

"Can we talk again? I'd really like to know what it is you saw."

"Can't ask anyone else can you?" he mumbled.

"No, no I can't," I replied. "How come you were left behind, Albert? What made you special?" I thought aloud. Maybe I could draw the conversation around via the *how* and onto the *what*.

The room had darkened despite the fluorescent light above, as if the storm were leaking through the window frame.

"I went mad," Albert stated.

My pen froze half way through a word.

He'd turned to face me, eyebrows raised, a tired smile revealing the man Albert had once been. I'm always ready for the conviction with which mad men speak and I'm unshaken by it. In their minds, what they see is real and true. But when the fisherman's brushed-steel gaze met mine, I saw nothing but reluctant sanity.

"I went barkin' loony crazy," Albert continued without a hint of humour. He shuffled around but stayed hidden behind his knees. "That's what saved me. When they ran, I stayed. When they screamed, I wa' quiet. When they fell, I wa' already on my knees. When they-"

The wrinkles on his brow realigned into a pattern of torture. There was something buried there, I could see it on his haggard face as plain as the suspect stains on his pyjamas. He began to weep in dry sobs, his body not able to spare the fluid.

Was Albert somehow responsible for Cormouth? Surely that was impossible.

His sobs died away. Now he shivered, shook his head as if dismissing reality. I let my fingers caress the file on the table beside me. Images taken by the police; transcripts of Albert's first incomprehensible statements; reports on what they'd found in Cormouth, or rather what they hadn't found.

Pinned to the inside cover were photographs of Albert himself. The first policeman on the scene had the foresight to make a record before an ambulance arrived.

In the first picture, Albert lay a little way off, crumpled on a wind-beaten beach. Wet sand piled against his body as if he were melting into the dunes.

Albert's form in the sand, discarded, a broken marionette.

A close-up of Albert's unconscious face, and the first time you can make out the sigils on his sand-powdered forehead.

A picture from inside the hospital. The police hadn't let the nurses remove the markings on his forehead and palms until they could fathom their origin. When archives gave nothing resembling them, it was assumed that they were of Albert's own design. The blood he'd used to draw them was his own, from a slash in his forefinger.

Albert's eyes in that photograph haunt me. Standing out from the darkness like a cat's; every shadow in the room collecting around his eyes and manic mouth, seeming to pour into his wrinkles like a viscous fluid. The deep scarlet design on his forehead. Crouched like a beast in his hospital gown, Albert was a man turned demon. Hard to believe that it was the same sorry figure I saw before me now, head buried in his arms.

I reached inside the manila folder and slid out the only picture without Albert in it. Aerial shots of the beach. Immense trenches had been scored into the wet sand. The lines were irregular, serpentine, leading down to the water's edge. The spot where Albert had been laid marked by a glowing yellow flag.

A realisation hit me with such force that I caught my breath.

"Albert-" I began, but stopped when I realised that my voice was shaking. I tried again, forcing resolve into every syllable. "Albert, who came out of the sea?"

He wouldn't raise his head or answer my questions.

My mouth ran dry.

The steady *whomp whomp whomp* of blood rose in my ears.

My shoes squeaked across the linoleum, the photograph dangling from my fingers. My shadow fell across Albert's foetal form. Against my better judgement, I crouched. With a gentle touch to his vibrating knee, I implored in a whisper, thirsty for answers but afraid of the fountain.

"Who came out of the sea, Albert?"

His head jerked upward. I fell back, landing heavily.

I hadn't heard it, but Albert had.

His face contorted; eyes widening, jaw dropped into a skull-like mask. A high-pitched keening came from his throat, like an animal trapped in pain.

With hands pressed to my ears, I still couldn't hear what Albert had heard. I scrambled for the door. Three burly orderlies shoved me back inside as they made for the crazed fisherman. Taking handfuls of his pyjamas, they lifted him bodily.

The last time I saw Albert he passed by me moving horizontally through the air, his body rigid with fear, whining and wailing like a banshee with a broken heart.

As the echoes of the bestial lament died away down the corridor, I took my seat to steady myself. The quivering in my heart slowly rested, my ears lost their ring, but the tremors in my hands wouldn't die. I wished that my glass of water didn't lay in a puddle on the floor. The photograph had fallen there in my panic, its corners beginning to curl in the fluid.

The room had a small sink backed by green tiles and dirty grout. I used it to splash my face, to drink from my hands. The water tasted like chalk. Between my pallid complexion and the tile's green glow, I looked ill.

I made to leave. The room seemed crowded, and my desire to escape back to the outside world grew stronger. Shuffling my notes into the file any-which-way, I finally heard what Albert had.

It was on the very edge of perception but must have sounded like Death's drum beat to Albert. It pounded on his fragile psyche until he could only take solace in his own head. I heard this softest sound and never have the hairs on my neck risen so high so fast.

Against the asylum's high windows, the storm's rain had begun to patter.

2

I SPAN AROUND, heckles raised.

Pebbles. Just pebbles scuttling in the wind.

My raised collar did nothing to stop the gale, so harsh it seemed to blister my skin. On the greyest stretch of English coastline in existence, Cormouth clung like a barnacle; pressed into the bedrock by a constant rolling thundercloud, hemmed by an unforgiving sea. The nearest town was over twenty miles inland. Except for this beach, anyone wanting access to land would need to scale sheer cliffs that crumbled like biscuit.

Cormouth was a museum to itself. No signs of a mass exodus could be found by the professionals, and who was I to contest their conclusions? Still, I'd come to Cormouth seeking answers on the word of a madman. I had a strong suspicion that I might just be "barking loony crazy" myself.

Cormouth made the national newspapers, the networks, and even international news to a certain degree. And that's what bothered me. With so many crazed enthusiasts of religion or cults, why hadn't someone come to Cormouth? There were no visitors, no candles or shrines to the lost; there had been no looting, nothing vandalised. The latter was my greatest surprise.

Every home was as it had been left. Belongings, clothes, food on tables. Every door was unlocked, and I'd already wandered through many of the rooms. I'd call it a ghost town, but I had a feeling that even ghosts would have left this place alone.

If all that could be believed, then why not the faint flare of Albert's sanity?

That look of his. It had convinced me that something happened here, on the very spot where I now stood on Cormouth beach; something that made Albert so afraid of water that he dehydrated himself to death. He'd done all that without telling me a single thing. All I needed was his eyes and the sound of his wail.

A gale whipped at the sand, occasionally lifting a cyclone of dancing grains. They peppered my matted hair and damp coat. There was nothing left to be seen of the enormous, serpentine trenches which had been here when Albert was found. The sea had taken them.

I've been to Auschwitz. I've stood in those long grey chambers. I've felt pressed on every side by the weight of the suffering which has lost none of its potency despite the years. Some people are moved to tears by it. Even someone naïve of the atrocities would feel it; an aura of anguish.

Similar could be said of Cormouth beach.

I didn't know what had happened there, what had happened to Albert. But by every primal instinct that linked us as human beings, I shared his fear. A sense of imminent finality, of ending, settled on me. It stripped away my civility, leaving me on the edge of what was left of my prehistoric nerves. I was a monkey, wary for the sound of predators I couldn't see.

A PART OF me wanted to stay away from Cormouth overnight, even though the sullen skies meant that sunlight never truly came. But another made me stay; Albert's part. I'd found his cabin, unpleasantly close to the sea, and decided to stay there. If I was ever going to find a solution to Cormouth's mystery, I'd need to stay as close to Albert's movements as possible. The constant duality in my mind screamed and argued that I should be away from this place, far away. I'm not sure if it was stupidity or resolve that made me take up bunk on Albert's living room floor.

The scent of wet rope and salt was everywhere.

There was little in the way of ornaments in the old fisherman's home. One of everything could be found. One plate, one cup, one fork. The opposite of the Seven Dwarves' cottage. No photographs, no trinkets, no letters from a bygone age. It was a vulgar place to exist. I felt like modern man stepping into the cave of a Neanderthal. There seemed little that could link me to Albert other than the inexplicable dread he'd infected me with.

I explored. Or rather I pried and snooped. That was the only reason I found the cellar door hidden beneath a rug made of sacking. I suppose stereotypes have to come from somewhere.

Where steps led down to a dank space beneath the house, I discovered why Albert's life above seemed so drab.

First, I found something that I didn't expect to be there. A light switch.

The wind hooted between double doors at one end of the room, setting the single bulb swinging. Shadows flowed and broke like waves on Albert's small fishing craft. A pair of wooden runners beneath the boat's hull would make it easy to slide out of the doors at high tide.

I wondered how close the water came to the other side of those doors.

Netting hung from the ceiling filled with all manner of nautical paraphernalia; none of which I understood the use of. To a man born and bred on dry land, this was a trove of unusual artefacts. The same might be said of Albert if I'd taken him to my office filled with books of psychiatric theory. As I pondered how a man enamoured by the sea could become so afraid of its primary ingredient, I shuffled around the room.

Between tins of *Gelcoat*, spools of line, and a host of floats that filled every inch of surface was an old ledger. Cardboard-bound and cover-stained, the book sat alone on Albert's makeshift workbench. Any other objects stood at a respectful distance. That I should find a book here seemed a miracle. I had to read it.

Taking the stool by Albert's workbench, I began to swipe aside tools and objects to make room.

Dammit.

The workbench, fashioned from a pair of old planks, struck out at me with a splinter. The wooden needle was wide and the force of my own hand drove it deep. I yanked, just wanting it to be out and swore under my breath. A healthy bloom of blood rose to the surface.

Outside, the wind had risen further, the doors now emitting an eerie howl that seemed endless. The temperature had dropped another few degrees, surely past freezing.

I sucked at my finger as I opened the scrapbook.

Not a single date or word was inscribed any-where. Drawings filled the pages, crammed into tight rows. The diagrams were stylised as in ancient Incan depictions; detailed but simplified. Beasts like nothing I could ever conceive merged with wailing and thrashing men and women. Tentacles or tails; masses of teeth and eyes seemed to make up the bodies of the creatures.

Thumbing through the ledger, I made sure I on-ly touched the edges so as not to wake the beasts that squirmed on the paper. Still, the blood from my pricked finger spilled more than once. I tried not to think about it but I was never comfortable leaving behind my life's fluid pressed between those hungry pages.

Albert must have been mad for a long time be-fore the end of Cormouth. I wondered if he was ridiculed by the townsfolk, called names by the children, or seen as the town's charge and humoured. These small communities tended to stick together. I certainly hoped that was the case for Albert. Still, how could a man create such a story in only pictures? The imagination it took, despite his madness, must have been exquisite. I would have liked to meet him before the twist of his mind.

The tale in the scrapbook rolled on. The humans stopped being eaten, at least so often. Many of them were depicted prostrate before the creatures. The thought struck me that Albert may have been illiterate. Was this the man's attempt at a novel of some fantasy? Lord of the Rings for those who couldn't read? The thought amused me, and I found myself comforted by it. If this was a work of fiction, there was nothing to fear. Nothing except the creeping sense that I was fooling myself.

The story seemed to come to an end abruptly with no real reason. There were simply no more pictures. I was compelled to find out what happened. The story had gripped me more than any literary work ever could. They say that humans thrive on material that scares them, for fear is just another type of excitement. Rollercoasters, horror movies, a scary book. My body was thrumming with fearful energy as if I'd done all three simultaneously.

At the back of the scrapbook, beyond the pages that Albert had never used, was a lump that told me something was hidden there. Another drawing, folded in four. It was, for the most part, blank. A single line writhed its way across the page. One word was inscribed above a swift circle.

Cormouth

It was Albert's drawing of the Cormouth coast, the circle marking home. Further along the coastline, around a bend in the crumbling cliffs, was another word.

Alice

Who was Alice? Could Albert have had a wife? And if so, what became of her?

3

OVERNIGHT, THE WIND had dropped to a chill breeze; the sea steadied to a tentative undulation. Storm clouds still blocked the sun's warmth and light. From my position on the cliff top I could see Cormouth to my right and the drop of the cliff in front and to my left.

My gloves worked the knot out of my neck. Albert's floorboards weren't the most comfortable place to sleep.

Fumbling at Albert's map with woollen fingers, I managed to open it up. Alice was here, somewhere here. I risked a stroll to the cliff edge, looking for some marker of burial. There was none.

The sea had receded, exposing dragon-spine rocks that footed the cliffs. The wind knocked loose boulders to be swallowed by the surf. The resounding crack of stone on stone and harsh battering of the sea assaulted the ears. I had no clue about tides or when they should rise and fall, but as I walked from Cormouth I had noticed the sea slowly being dragged away from land.

It seemed that luck was on my side. With the sea

pulled back from the rocks, I could see where Alice lay.

I should have done more research before stepping out; I should have searched again through the few photos I'd found in Albert's home. I should have tried to find documents with Alice's name on them. But I hadn't. With thoughts of the scrapbook and the images it contained, of Albert and the blood-sigils decorating his body, I was swamped with a desire to find Alice wherever she may be. I'd rushed out, unprepared.

Wedged between the rocks with sea foam slipping down her broken sides, Alice lay beaten.

I ran. Seeking a way down to the beach, I scuttled along a worn path and down to the sand. Cormouth disappeared from sight beyond the cliff.

I stopped. As my feet met the beach, a sweat took me. My mouth flooded with saliva as if I were about to vomit. I pawed at my clothes in an effort to release them, almost dropping to my knees. Finally my scarf fell away and the toggles on my jacket released. I let the sea spray prickle my skin as I gulped down great lungfuls of air.

My throat dried to a crisp by the ambient salt, I coughed and coughed until I could do nothing but hold my aching ribs and ignore the line of drool that came from my mouth.

I've never felt so ill. My face seemed swollen;

baking hot.

But it passed. Slowly I regained my constitution and felt the cold once more. I remained doubled over but fastened my jacket. My scarf had blown away and I took a slow stroll to retrieve it. It rolled and slid along the ground at the breeze's will, drawing me away from the cliffs. Finally I snatched it from the ground and shook loose the sand.

WET SAND SUCKED at my shoes as I hugged the cliff, making toward the rocks where I clambered with hands and feet, never once finding a flat place to rest.

A grinding crack.

Shards of stone peppered me.

My shoes sent me slithering down into a foaming mouth between the rocks. Seaweed grasped my jacket and water soaked into my trouser bottoms. Another piece of the cliff had fallen from above to be pulverised not fifteen feet from where I crouched. Plastered to my face like the seaweed on my shoes, I brushed my hair aside for the hundredth time. With the sound of battering waves, brine blinded me. I spat out a mouth full of salt.

This was ridiculous. What was I doing out there, alone? This was how people died. There would be no coastguard or lucky coincidence to send a heroic dog walker my way. I should have gone back. And I would have gone back if I hadn't seen Alice.

An errant wave draped her body with foamy lace. Water leaked out through a gaping wound in her side. She'd collected a shroud of seaweed and a starfish clung to her slender frame. Pieces of her hull were scattered around her like dropped firewood.

Although she'd been driven across the stone spines to her death, there was still too much precarious ground to cover if I wanted to touch her. I turned away, wondering why I'd let myself be drawn here for a glimpse of another man's wreck.

I checked the cliff face for falling rocks, and made back toward dry land. I must have walked past the cave on my way to Alice, but I hadn't seen it. Unless you stood where I did then, facing as if returning to the beach from the wrecked boat, a crease in the cliff's side hid the dark entrance entirely.

I saw it as Albert must have, and followed in footsteps once again.

4

I'VE NEVER BEEN the type of person to seek out a gym; I've certainly never been a gymnast. Crouching and twisting to enter the cave's entrance, every part of me complained. At first I wondered how Albert had managed this same entrance and realised with horror that he probably did it better.

Night comes fast and unexpectedly in Cormouth. Fogs rise like dough at the slightest whim of the weather. That's why I already had the torch in my jacket.

The ground inside the cave's entrance sloped upward, and I had to stay crouched to move along the passage. Wet grit, deposited as the tide infiltrated the cliff each day, crunched beneath my feet. I probably didn't have long here. If I found myself trapped by the tide, it was doubtful there was another exit.

As I climbed, the silt slowly gave way to a smooth stone floor and I could stand upright. Looking back toward the entrance, it became obvious that the passageway had been crafted. The walls were too smooth, the slope too regular.

I must have climbed steadily for a good fifteen minutes before the cave opened up. Even then the weak light of my torch didn't reach the other side. Taking three steps forward, searching the ground for chasms or footfalls, my torch touched water. A pool occupied at least a little of the chamber floor.

I didn't step to the edge, but returned to the wall instead.

My hand trailed along the stone and I slowly allowed myself to believe the room had been made as the passage had. The surface was too even, too perfectly shaped for it to be otherwise. Still, I wouldn't let myself think about who would carve such a place deep in a seaward cliff.

I almost fell.

I'd been staring into the dark, my mind wandering so far that I'd stopped checking the ground for obstacles. In my puddle of torch light was a gift from Albert.

A cable.

I dared to follow it away from the wall, risking losing my bearings. My curiosity was making me a risk-taker. If this had been a day only a week ago, I would never have to come to Cormouth to begin with, never mind clamouring out onto the rocks or exploring some long-forgotten cave. Long forgotten except for Albert, of course.

The wire snaked upwards through the air for a few inches as if floating, and there was the plug, and the generator. I don't think I hesitated a second. In this place, lost in time, such a modern thing as electricity melted any qualms I'd normally have.

After only one false start, the generator reacted to my prodding and fired into life.

All around the room, lamps flickered alight.

5

THE CHAMBER WAS circular and far more vast than I could have imagined in the dark. The pool took up the entire centre of the room. It couldn't have been as deep as it appeared. It looked as if water had been lifted from the depths of the ocean and planted here, bringing an impenetrable darkness with it. Thoughts of what might lay below made trickles of sweat run down my collar.

I turned, instead, to the walls.

All along the smooth surface, faded and peeling in places, were row upon row of paintings. It took no genius to recognise them. I walked around the room, maybe ten times or more, reading the story without words. Where Albert's ledger had ended, the walls continued. Men and women farmed crops, built homes and even fished from rafts in great teams.

A small group of men appeared, all wearing white robes. Whenever the creatures of tentacle and teeth emerged, so did they. The men in white presided over the sacrifices of women and children.

I found myself checking over my shoulder.

The pool sat defiantly still.

Despite the generator's steady chug, I could hear the gentle lapping of the pool's shores.

Trying desperately to ignore it I stayed engrossed in the wall paintings. Such a vibrant depiction of life for these people and the Gods they worshipped. I thought of Albert, a man of the sea, finding this place. Coupled with his seaside superstitions and old tales of beasts beneath the waves (maybe some latent schizophrenia) Albert had started to believe. He copied the paintings, studied them, but had never spoken of them to others. If he had, Cormouth would have become an archaeological Mecca over night. Albert had managed to find something unheard of in the scientific world. An ancient civilisation that thrived on the coasts of England.

The story changed again.

A woman appeared. A woman in red clothing.

With the woman at their head, masses of men and women were shown marching to the sea with spears and shields. The creatures were set upon; the men in white cast into the sea. At some point in their history, this ancient people had stopped believing in their Gods.

With the Red Lady at their head once more, the people were shown with carts, children and horses all headed in the same direction. In the distance, on the final picture, a row of trees.

The generator popped and chugged, setting the lights flickering for a moment. Its dial told me it was nearly out of fuel. I'd waited too long. If it was possible, the pool seemed to have crept further into the chamber. Ink-black water now licked the generator's feet where there had been none before. I panicked. The tide must be rising and I had to reach the exit before I was trapped entirely.

FAR TOO LATE.

The sea poured into the cave in pulses. Water

flooded toward my feet as I watched. I retreated back into the chamber. The generator was giving some disconcerting chugs now. I debated briefly whether to turn it off and save what was left of its power, but decided against it. If it shut down now, it might never come back on.

I checked my pocket. The torch was still there. I'd need it soon, no doubt, and I swore at myself for not bringing spare batteries. Still, if I'd had the forethought necessary for this entire trip, a laden donkey would have had to carry the equipment. I searched the walls once more, while there was still light.

Though the pool slithered further into the room, it never met the walls. I could see from the line of deposited sand on the ground and a lack of water marks on the walls. Priding myself on my Holmes-esque ingenuity, I set myself down to wait out the night.

I WOKE IN such darkness that it laid heavy on my chest. I sucked in one thick breath, fumbling for the torch beside me. It was gone. I was left in the darkness with only the lapping of water for company. I winced as nothing touched my outstretched foot.

The torch. It had to be somewhere!

In my panic, I almost sent the torch skidding out into the darkness. It had rolled only a few inches from where I'd left it, but enough to cause panic. I tore off my gloves to click on the switch.

At the edge of the thin beam, water ebbed and flowed not inches from where my feet had been. As the tide rose outside, so did the chamber's pool.

Somewhere in that pool stood the generator, now empty, silent. I would have poured my life's blood into it for the sake of a little light. I checked my watch. It was early in the morning, just after midnight. I tried to remember what I knew of the moon and tides. How long would it take for the tide to retreat? Could I be here for hours? I was certain the torch wouldn't hold out that long. And when the time came to leave, could I find my way to the exit in the dark?

Reluctantly, I turned off the torch. I would need the battery for my escape.

SOMEWHERE IN THE darkness, a sound woke me. My head jerked upward, slamming into the stone and setting my ears ringing.

Outside, sea battered rock. The chamber was filled with echo upon echo of booming and cracking noise.

Phlap.

In a space between the crashing waves, I heard it. The sound of wet movement.

Boom after boom deafened me. I tried to strain

my ears past the din.

It came again.

A small sound like the thrash of an eel on stone.

I wriggled away, forcing my shoulder blades into the wall, trying to remove myself from the pool's edge. My feet slid on grit. In a momentary break from the racket outside, the minute crunch was enhanced to an avalanche by the darkness.

There was the scrape of sand from across the chamber.

I sat perfectly still, holding my breath, clutching the blind torch to my chest.

I held my breath as long as I could, letting out only a shuddering breath when my body screamed for it, and prayed that the sounds of high tide would drown it out.

There was only the smell of salt.

No sound. No movement.

Something touched my shoe.

I almost screamed. Biting down on my lip, I tried not to move. Adrenalin pounded until I was senseless. Writhing tentacles filled my skull.

The beat of the sea was my heart; the rocks my crumbling mind.

The cave's freezing air sucked at my breath, making me pant.

Nothing grasped for me out of the darkness.

Every time a wave met the cliff, I flinched, covering my ears. Soon I was curled against the chamber's wall, arms over my head.

I made a shaky pact with myself that imagination was the key. I had obviously been woken from a dream, the movement of the pool seeming louder than it was. This darkness, this chamber; they rendered me a child. But I didn't call for mother. I didn't light the torch.

A small part of me was happy not to see what might be searching the darkness with cold limbs.

6,

I MUST HAVE fallen asleep again. There was something about the salty air, how it tightened my skin, that made me so tired. Or maybe it was the fresh air. I'd been thinking of my mother without realising it. She always told me that fresh air made you tired.

I don't know where the courage came from, but I lit the torch.

The pool had pulled away from me; the tide was low.

I moved as quickly as the dark would allow. With one hand on the wall, torch searching the ground, I circumvented the room.

I stopped.

There, in my path, in the sand, serpentine lines scored into the sediment.

My torch followed them, down to the pool's

edge.

My god, I ran; stumbling over myself in the gloom, torch flashing across the ground, the walls, striking the pool in flares.

When the wall disappeared, I almost fell.

The passage took me down and down.

And, eventually, daylight peeked in through the cave's entrance.

As the light grew, I think I ran harder. I can't really remember, but I was soon scrambling out over the rocks.

I ONLY STOPPED running once free of the beach. My throat was dry, my mouth tasted like tin. Scurrying up the cliff's slope, distancing myself from the sea, I let myself rest for a while.

Wind deafened me, making noises in my ears that weren't there, but had me searching over my shoulder time and time again. I sat on the grassy cliff top, letting the dew soak into me. I shivered but didn't care.

I wanted rid of that place; I'd had enough.

Nothing of the night would come back to me. Nothing of paintings, markings on the ground or the midnight sounds would replay. I sat dumb to the world.

Clouds fought each other for dominion of the sky. Below, waves tested the cliffs for weakness as if seeking to eradicate the land.

BY THE TIME I reached town, the sun had found a gap between clouds and horizon, spearing light across the sea and painting thundercloud underbellies with red. Cormouth was bathed in flame-light. Walking down the main street's gentle slope, I had to shield my eyes.

Every doorway and window glared; cracks in stone and mortar made grins and gaping mouths until every house in Cormouth seemed to be tasting, laughing, sneering. There was no doubt that I had to leave. My car was parked on the outskirts of town and I intended to drive it as fast I could; to play deafening music until that sea, that wind and that god-forsaken place were far behind. I just had to collect my things from Albert's cabin.

I don't know what I'd expected to find there, what answers, what reasons for Albert's madness. There was nothing but ghosts and paranoia. Empty homes that would never see life again, waiting for the wind to break their windows and open doors until inside was the outside. Roofs would let the moon and rain into halls and bathrooms. Grass would replace carpets, sand would pile in living room corners. Beds and chairs would stand like the skeletons of ships.

I shouldered Albert's door and swept through the

living room collecting my few belongings, wandering in circles so that I never had to stand still. With my duffle bag full, I checked my pocket for car keys and finally stopped with my hand on the door.

What was the point of this? Not the leaving; I knew deep down and high up why I was leaving, but to leave with nothing would be pointless. Dropping my bag at the door, I made for the cellar. I never wanted to see Cormouth again, or even speak of it if it could be helped, but someone might. What Albert had found in those caves was nothing short of incredible. At the very least I should take his book to show someone.

The stairs creaked as I descended; the wind hooted. Sunset bled in through the ill-fitting seaward doors. If I wanted to be out by nightfall, I'd have to hurry.

I sat at Albert's workbench, taking in the taste of the air, and couldn't help but open the book. I thumbed the pages like a child's flick book cartoon. Pictures of people fluttered along, giving them movement.

Something pounded the cellar's doors with such force that I let the book fall from the bench as I span around.

The room had gone momentarily dark but sunset slowly faded back through the cracks.

I couldn't move; had no idea what was happening.

The doors rattled again, the light blocked out.

It came again. The doors strained on their hinges and settled back; the light obstructed by some great bulk. A chain hung across the doors clanked and shivered.

Again. Again.

The last red light of day dying and flaring like a beacon as I crawled back until the workstation dug painfully into my spine.

The sound was incredible, like the sea was screaming somewhere beyond those doors. I clasped arms over ears. Light pulsed with every strike that shook the cellar. Nets above swung and jostled, water leaked in under the doors and sea wind danced around the room.

The book lay open on the ground, thrashing limbs and writhing beasts coursed across the pages. Screams seemed just beyond hearing; the roar of battle. Above them all, the voice of a woman in red calling out words I didn't understand. If the pounding would only stop, I was sure I could hear them.

The doors were buckling, the chain straining its rusted links.

I must have screamed, but the sound of sea and wind, the hammering of wood, drowned it out. I fell to my knees, folding myself until my forehead touched the ground. The din never stopped long enough for my ears to recover.

I couldn't hear, couldn't think.

I screamed silently.

To the sound of splintering wood and a final blast of scarlet sunset, I passed out.

7

I WOKE, SPRAWLED on the workshop floor. Shreds of the seaward doors hung from their hinges; shards of wood peppered the room.

My extremities were blue and salt crystallised on my stubble. I hugged myself, willing body heat to return.

My legs forced me up in jerks. Most of the workshop's oddments were strewn on the floor. Upturned pots left sticky puddles that had collected fishing lures like flies in treacle. I fumbled my way along, holding on to the wall. The workbench had been torn from the wall, and now lay upturned against an opposing wall. Touching my head, I found a tacky mass where it had hit me.

There was no way I was getting out by the stairs. Something had smashed them, snapping each sturdy beam in half. The doors to the beach were the only option.

Stepping over the threshold, I came down to the wet sand.

Albert's little boat littered the sand, its hull torn

to toothpicks.

Trenches scored in the shore, decorated with seaweed bunting, led up from the water's edge. Looking out across the mess of flayed sand, slick green and splintered wood, I felt sick. My legs threatened to fail me. But the algae-slick wall of Albert's home held me up. Where Cormouth's road met the sand I hurried upward, away from the beach, the sea. Past destitute homes, a darkened village shop, a town hall. Up and out of Cormouth.

My car was still there, leaning where I'd bumped it onto a grass verge.

I managed to turn the key, and crank the heat.

EXHAUST FUMES, TURNED to smoke signals by the cold, attracted attention.

As the engine sputtered on the last drop of petrol, a police officer on her way past Cormouth found me slumped across the passenger seat.

For a week I endured hospital rations and psychological probes. I told them nothing about sounds in the dark, of slithering trails or pounding doors. I was exhausted, they said, dehydrated and hypothermic. They said I was lucky to have been found on such a remote road. They said I shouldn't have gone alone.

I nodded, thanked them, and ate the largest portion of Humble Pie I could stomach. I was just fascinated by the case, I said. I had to know.

They smiled, and nodded as if I'd said the right thing, and told me my dedication was honourable.

Albert's book has been found, and taken away. Archaeologists probe the cave chamber by day, but never stay beyond high tide. Ruins have been uncovered where Cormouth used to be, all along the cliff top and to the beach below. They say a significant discovery has been made; enough to make the world forget about an abandoned fishing village that once stood there.

I suggested they credit Albert.

The Fly Man

THE SOUND OF screaming metal.

    Glass falling in every direction.

Philip's voice, lost in a storm of sound.

Pulsing light.

SOMEWHERE BEYOND PHILIP'S darkness, a strong perfume lingered and faded. Underneath, the tang of detergent, of lemons. A scent of overpowering cleanness.

Pressure. A sensation on his arm that tightened until his hand was numb. A circle of ice on his chest that moved here, then here, then here across his heart. Jesus, there was pain. Pain in his toes that he couldn't retreat from. A muffled sound came in bursts, intonation without words that could only be a distant voice. A rumble. A man.

Blistering light.

Pain behind Philip's unflinching eye. His first sight of the white expanse. A muted shape passing across, a flash one side, then the other. Darkness, and the man's voice again.

✕

SOMEWHERE BEYOND THE darkness, that perfume. A muffled sound, higher, softer.

Something was in Philip's mouth. Holding down his tongue, filling his throat. His chest swelled and shrank. When he tried to breathe against it, it hurt. His back was pressed to something. No, something was taking his weight. There was light in the darkness, just a little. A thick red veil filtered most of it, but there was enough that he saw the shadow pass to his right. That perfume. The light blocked out and a voice speaking sweetly.

Philip's world slid sideways. The room as he understood it span like a fairground teacup. Pain in his legs. Bone-deep agony that shot through a hip and into his spine. Something…something else pressing into his…

Jesus.

Philip screamed at the dark.

✕

A PRESSURE ON his hand. Soft, warm, pleasant.

Something that squeezed and then was wet.

Sarah.

"…on his own now, so we can get rid of some of these machines."

"Is there anything, anything at all?"

"Not yet. But it hasn't been very long. Just because we haven't seen any improvement doesn't mean there won't be any."

"Oh God, I hope so."

"That being said, you realise-"

"I know, I know."

THE WHITE EXPANSE had lines in it. Squares. Tiles.

Philip turned toward the light without moving. Casting his eyes to their farthest corners, he saw half of a window to one side. The tip of a bouquet to the other. Above was a plastic headboard. Only the transparent ghost of his nose below.

The hush of a door on linoleum. The perfume. He'd finally see who it was. Footsteps around the bed, one shoe squeaked. Humming. It was a woman. Eventually she slid into view. Head and shoulders only, but she stood over him.

"Oh my God," she said. "You're awake!"

Philip tried to speak.

How long?

"Now, there's nothing to worry about, Philip.

You've had a bad accident."

How long?

"You're in hospital. We're looking after you."

Where's Sarah?

"I'll go get the doctor so that he can see you awake. I'll be back in a minute. Do you want to sit up a little? You can't see much from down there."

The bed began to move, propelling him forward like a mummy in an old movie.

That pain. His legs. His back.

Stop. Please.

As the horizon dropped, the white expanse slid out of view to be replaced by a section of wall. A board with his name, a clock. A unit of drawers. Where the parallels of Philip's legs should have been was a sheet-covered box. They were still there, he could feel them. Hot and rigid like twin pokers fresh from the fire.

Jesus. The pain.

"There we go. I'll be right back."

The woman, the nurse, rushed out, her shoe squeaking like a rusty bicycle.

The room was silent. Only the nurse's fading perfume remained, cool sunlight, and shards of agony buried deep in Philip's wrecked body.

The door again. Philip watched the nurse hold it open and the man swoop in.

"Ah! We're very pleased to see you awake

Mr…oh my god."

"What is it, Doctor?"

"Look at his eyes, Anika. This man is in agony. Who sat him up?"

"Well-"

"Lay him down, quickly. I'll get him something."

The horizon rose like the sides of a listing ship. Philip's pain eased to a shattering throb and the white expanse spread out before him. There was the swish of the door, feet, and a tugging at his arm. Something ran cold under his skin.

Then the darkness.

✕

"I'M AFRAID NOT. We sedated him while we control the pain. To be honest, we didn't really expect him to wake up so soon. Oh yes, I'd say it was a good sign."

Philip opened his eyes to the white expanse. The strip of neon light down its centre was out now. Sunlight came through the window, warming the right side of his body. Something to his right, a slight pressure on his left hand. Soft, warm, pleasant. Philip swung his eyes that way. The room span and blurred as if he were moving through syrup.

Sarah.

She was there. Although her eyes were only slits in the surrounding red, and leaked constantly, they opened wide when he looked at her.

"Phil? It's so good to see you awake," she said, and stood so that he wasn't straining to see her. She wavered as if stood inside a heat wave. Philip blinked his eyes to clear them, but that just made it worse. Sarah was only a blur now. Her voice seemed far off.

What did they give me?

His stomach churned and his head as lined with cotton. Sarah was still talking, asking a question, but the cotton wouldn't let him hear. She squeezed his hand and he tried to smile but couldn't tell if his face moved. He swung his eyes away from her and around the room.

A dark figure stood at the end of his bed.

Philip's heart rate leapt, setting the heart monitor pipping.

Oh my god, what did they give me?

The figure stood perfectly still, but its edges shifted as if it were made of smoke. Still, it seemed more real than Sarah's distant pleas. She was shaking his shoulder but it might as well have been someone else's.

His eyes felt hot, as if looking at the dark man burnt, but Philip couldn't look away.

The door banged in its jamb. Sarah was gone.

Don't. Don't leave me alone with him!

The nurse burst back in. She ran around the bed, through the figure, and paid him never mind. Sarah was by his side again.

The shadow was gone.

Philip's eyes rolled as the sedative kicked in.

✕

"He looked so scared."

"We can only guess at how the pain killers are affecting his damaged brain. But without them, he'd be in agony. We could put him in a chemical-induced coma, make sure he's suffering no ill effects from the medication and give his brain time to recover on its own."

"But I only just got him back."

"I know. But this way, we stand a better chance of not unduly taxing his system."

✕

Philip opened his eyes and saw the room. The neon strip above reflected from every white surface, making flares of light in his watery eyes. He blinked them away. Someone had sat him up and left. But the pain wasn't there. And the room didn't swim.

The bedclothes were folded aside, exposing his shins. Dots of old blood still showed where the pins had been. His feet were pale, almost tallow, and they curved in as if the soles were trying to meet. Although they couldn't move, he could tell they were stiff as wood. But at least the frames and pins were gone. And the pain.

His eyes snapped to the left. There had been a shadow. But it was beyond frosted glass. Just someone passing by. He settled down again.

Outside the window it was night. Philip remembered the last time he knew it was night. He remembered kissing Sarah, and setting off for work. He remembered the streetlights making reflected comets on the windshield.

His head ached. He tried not to remember any more.

Somewhere beyond his thoughts, a sound assailed him. A hum. No, a drone. It wasn't the motion of the air mattress' motor. Most of the other machines were gone now. Philip cast his eyes as far as they would stretch to find the source. But it came to him. It skimmed his ear, setting his teeth on edge and was gone again. A tiny black speck that span and dipped through the air.

Damn fly.

It made coils in the air, climbing to the neon strip like Icarus, buzzing angrily when it hit the light's plastic cover, and came down twirling like a shot spitfire. Philip thought of laughing, but knew he didn't have the control to make it a reality.

But the fly wasn't beaten. It was back. It tested the window's strength, butting time and again against the glass, each time with a frustrated buzz. Philip sat and watched it until the monotonous plink and buzz of the insect grated on his nerves.

Just give it up, for God's sake. You're done. You're dying in here with me and that's it.

But the fly kept on.

Plink, buzz. Plink, buzz.

You're driving me nuts. Stop it, will you?

Plink, buzz.

Then nothing. No hum. No plink. No buzz. Philip's ears seemed to ring in the silence.

✕

A PRICKLE ON his forearm woke him. Such a tiny sensation. The rising of a hair maybe, or a slightest breeze.

It was still night, or maybe the night after. The room was still the same. Only the clock had moved.

The prickle again.

Philip looked down at his arm. The fly. Or maybe another, but to him it was the same. He flinched his wrist to dispel it, but nothing happened.

Of course. Of course you won't move. Dammit.

The fly danced a circle on his skin, sending nauseous sensations across Philip's body. Now it was closer, he could see sapphire between its coarse hairs, a little jewel with crystal wings.

Get off me, damn you. Who knows whose shit

you've been sitting on?

The fly rubbed its hands together, only a vacant look in its eyes. Then it went for a stroll in its warm pink garden. Philip's arm crawled under its feet; he tried to grit his teeth and realised that he could. But that little miracle wasn't enough to take his attention from the fly. It walked the length of his arm in curlicues until it reached the hem of his hospital gown. Philip's eyes strained to see the fly pause on the doorstep to this cave before walking in as if he owned the place.

Get out. Get out of there. Don't make yourself at home, you little bastard. Don't you dare.

Now out of sight, the fly seemed to be stamping its feet. Philip could feel the creep of its little legs as intense as pinpricks on his bicep.

Oh my god. I'm going to go mad. Please. Please leave me alone.

The fly reappeared as if he'd heard Philip's thoughts and, finding himself with room to stretch, took to his wings.

Philip watched it sail past the window as his panting settled, then come around the room, a darker speck against the black. He followed it across the bedside cabinet where it avoided the sweet flowers as only an ignorant fly can, and above the foot of his bed where the black figure waited.

Philip's heart jolted as if from his chest, enough

to send his flaccid body into painful spasm. Without the medication, the figure was only clearer. It was made of shadows held together by a tattered cowl. Here and there, he could see where the material had faded with wear to only a charcoal shade of its original black. This time it wasn't still. Philip could see that it breathed, or acted as if it were. The cowl rippled with breath. The fly flew a dizzy halo around its head before disappearing into the darkness beneath.

Philip screamed, and made no sound.

"HE'S DOING QUITE well. We think he may be in some discomfort with the splints, but we'll increase them slowly so that we don't put him in too much discomfort."

"How long will it take?"

"A while, I'm afraid."

"And what about himself? He doesn't seem to be improving."

"I know. But these things take time. According to the latest scan, there's still a lot of swelling and we don't want to force our hand. Patience is all we can have, and let it go down on its own."

"I'm sorry, I know I'm being impatient. I just want him back."

"It's alright. It's perfectly understandable."

✕

Philip snapped open his eyes, and quickly searched the room. He was alone, really alone. And cold enough to shiver. His feet ached as if he'd done a ten-mile hike. They were pressed into plastic moulds of some kind, woolly straps forcing his ankles down. But the throb in his head was worse. It pulsed behind his temples like a beacon. The skin around his eyes felt tight as if someone had pinned his ears to the pillow. He groaned, and was amazed when a gasp escaped. But it wasn't a good sound. It rattled. He could feel a thickness in his chest that made it hard to breathe. He tried to cough, to clear whatever it was, but groaned instead. Something lodged low in his throat, making him gag. He finally coughed, his shoulders juddering with the effort and his throat cleared. But he took no comfort in it. It was just reflex. His eyes watered enough to stream until he could taste salt on his cracked lips.

He smelled the nurse before he saw her. She bustled in and around his bed without looking at him and began rifling somewhere at his side. Only when she turned to take his temperature did she realise he was awake.

"Oh! Were you watching me?" she laughed. She laid a hand across her chest as if flattered. Philip couldn't help noticing how her uniform strained at the zip. And there was a stain on her collar, some fluid dried to yellow. Her fingernails had been red a few days ago, but the pink of her fingers was starting to show through the wear.

I'd like to watch you drown in that damned perfume if I had the chance.

He laughed, but only let out a gasp.

"Awww, are you trying to talk to me? You're so sweet."

If anything's going to make me crazy, it'd be you.

"Do you mind if I take your temperature? The doctor thinks you might have a chest infection. We don't want you developing a temperature, do we?"

Yes, I do mind. Don't you have monkeys that can do it? I'd prefer them.

The nurse pinched his ear, lifting it, and inserted the thermometer. It gave a small beep and was removed.

"You're warm," said the nurse, and starting pulling back his blankets.

No I'm not, I'm freezing. Are you mad? Put those back.

Adding insult to injury, she turned the fan on his bedside table so that it wafted across his face.

"I'll come check on you in five minutes when you've cooled down."

There was no point trying to talk her out of it. Philip was too occupied with the shaking that had started in his limbs. It felt good to have them moving, but the rapidity and lack of control scared him.

The nurse didn't come back.

✕

"How could you let him get sick? This is a hospital. People are supposed to get better here."

"It's fairly common for people who spend all their time in bed to contract pneumonia. Normally our body's secretions move as we walk around, clearing the lungs automatically. But between Philip's immobility and his inability to swallow properly, fluid has collected in his lungs and become infected."

"I bet it was that nurse. She's useless. She fumbles around, talking sweetly and making cups of tea, but she has no idea how to look after Philip. No idea."

"We'll know more after this course of antibiotics. Try not to worry."

✕

Philip's eyes rolled open like blinds letting light into his brain. His eyelids felt thick and heavy. He could smell his own breath like the underside of a compost heap. The rattle in his chest came with every inhalation. Someone must have left the heat on. His skin prickled like sunburn. A long clear tube ran from a suspended bag into his left arm. The drip drip drip in the bag's chamber pounded in time with his head.

Sarah. I think I'm ill.

But she wasn't there. There was only Philip, and the Fly Man.

Oh please, God, no.

It stood at the foot of his bed, fading in and out as Philip struggled to keep his eyes open. In the space of a laden blink, it was closer, almost pressing itself against the bed end. Philip groaned.

What do you want? Tell me what you want.

The figure leant forward, the darkness shifting beneath the cowl like trapped coal smoke. There was buzzing. Faint. Just beyond the rush of blood in Philip's ears. It grew to a hum as the figure leaned closer. The dark man extended something wrapped in the folds of its cloak, a hand maybe. Reaching out. Philip tried to retract his feet in their plastic casings, screaming at his nerves to obey. Panting, the heaviness in his chest was like a hand pressing him to the bed. He screamed in his head but the dark visitor couldn't hear it anymore than the nurse or Sarah could.

Philip's foot finally disappeared into the dark material. It was cold. So cold that his body snapped into spasm, forcing his shoulders and heels into the mattress, lifting his body from the bed. His fingers jerked back from the palm and the hands back from the wrists, muscles straining, each trying to escape its neighbour. But the pain was nothing compared to the sensation creeping along Philip's leg.

The buzzing was too loud for Philip to comprehend, a wall of constant sound. From the figure's cowl, flies came tumbling like a torrent of opals. They spilled over Philip's shin as thick as oil, and began to squirm their way toward his knee. Philip's spasm released like a gunshot, leaving him twisted on the bed. He was shivering hard enough to set his fingers playing some invisible piano; hard enough that his teeth slammed together as if on pistons. He tried to close his eyes, but found the sensation was too much to bear. So he watched. He watched as the flies smothered his pale skin. Spreading across his groin, his stomach and began to smother his arms. Then he couldn't see, but the flies were below his chin, he could feel them. He could only see the figure at his feet, shivering with anticipation at Philip's smothering.

The flies were on his face now, crawling over his lip and filling his mouth like black sand. His cheeks squirmed under a thousand little feet. Philip didn't try to scream. He cast his eyes to the white expanse as it faded into darkness.

A SINGLE DIGITAL tone that pierced the ears.
A sense of falling in every direction.
A pulse hammered into Philip's chest.
And Sarah's soft weeping in the dark.

Hunting Grounds

WORKING AT THE coffee shop is my perfect job. For one, the hours work around my uni course. For two, it's easy (once you remember what all the little cups are for). Three, I'm good at it. Some people are musicians, some great writers of literature. Even hung over or knackered from a night of cramming, or maybe even because I suffer so frequently from both, I make a mean coffee.

But the best part is the smell. From the first espresso, the bitter tang of roasting beans is so strong that it drowns out every other scent.

Java is my refuge.

The lunchtime rush was in full force. A hundred people wanting coffee and a toasted Panini, and I was the gatekeeper to their half hour of freedom. Beyond that stream of strangers checking their watches, Natalie walked in.

Dipping into the muffin case, my plastic tongs

hung empty. The *scorggle-orgle-orgle* of the Brasilia faded into the distance. If it weren't for Denver nudging me, a day's worth of confectionary would have been ruined by my untamed drool.

"Dream-girl's here," he said. I didn't really hear him but the nudge woke me up.

Natalie huffed the cold out of her hands and stamped her feet, the bobble of her hat dancing along. I've seen a thousand people do that. All day, every day. Stamp and huff, stamp and huff in the heater's dry belch. But Natalie made it a jig, like being cold was something to be happy for.

For once, I wished I could smell something other than coffee. I wondered if her toothpaste was spearmint or peppermint. What fabric softener did she use? Was she Mountain Fresh or Japanese Orchid? If it weren't for the coffee, I'd have been able to tell.

Before I could wonder anymore, Natalie slid into the queue and my present customer commanded attention.

"Buddy, you making love to that muffin or what?"

My throat tightened, a brief rumble escaping my lips. I hid it as a frog in my throat, and smiled.

"Sir, if I was, I'd have been done in seconds," I said.

The customer moved down the counter, grumping through his sculpted goatee. Feeling the complaint averted, I scratched behind my ear. It's a soothing habit. The next customer looked at me like I had fleas, so I made a point of changing my gloves. She seemed satisfied with that. I'm not sure why. Those gloves are useless; made from some kind of paper/plastic hybrid flattened out to a molecule's thickness. Denver said he'd once tested them with a very scientific scratch-and-sniff method; scratching something smelly with the glove and then sniffing his finger to ascertain carry-through. Playing with smells isn't my idea of a good time. Denver, however, honestly believes these little experiments are both ground breaking and of great worth to the human race.

I tended the queue on autopilot, order, serve, order, serve: "Thank you, have a nice day," whether I meant it or not.

Until Natalie stood at the counter.

"Cappuccino, please."

I'd heard it a million times but never so eloquent. And she actually smiled as if someone existed beyond the counter, not just something human-shaped to put your coins on.

"Um, yeah, sure," I said.

Not a good first line. I turned to the Brasilia and let my hands take over. My mouth was suddenly full of saliva as if I'd sniffed a roast ham. Every hair follicle tingled to attention. I forced it back, and worked on something witty to say.

"That'll be three fifty, please."

I doubt it'll go down in Movie History, but it was the best I could do at short notice. Natalie handed me the three fifty in exact change, not giving me another attempt at wooing her.

Sat near the window, the delicate bow of her lip caressed the cup. I must have sighed, because Denver nudged me.

"Don't bother," he said. "There's nothing you have that she wants, dude."

I didn't say anything. I didn't even register the boiling milk until it was too late.

"Damn it!"

I recoiled, clasping my hand. I nearly knocked Denver across the counter.

"Woah, man. Chill out!"

The skin had bubbled. I stared down, biting it back. Far too late. All around the blister and spreading across the back of my hand, the hair was coming. In thirty seconds my arm would look like a pissed off porcupine.

Everyone was looking. Denver. The customers. From her table by the window, Natalie was looking too. We caught eyes briefly as I snatched the first aid kit and ducked into the back room.

Bracing my hands between tight knees, I panted

as if in labor. And when that didn't work, I lifted the hand to my mouth. With long strokes, I licked the blister and the hair around it; the coolness of my saliva soothed the stinging. After a while the pain subsided leaving only the taste of damp fur.

The whole arm hadn't flared, just the hand. So as Denver came out back, I was able to cover the hair with a bandage.

"Dude, she'll want you even less if you're mutilated."

"I don't think that's possible."

"Come on, butt-wipe. There's some hungry suits out here that don't give a shit about your hand. I'll help you fill out the forms later. We'll tell them the Brasilia spat at you. You might even get some money out of it."

"Cheers."

Natalie was gone when we got back out, but the queue wasn't. It was longer, and fatter near the door where people were uncertain where to join.

Jenny finally arrived, two hours later than she should have. Without a word, still tying the strings on her apron, she started taking orders. Me and Denver dished out coffees and muffins; sandwiches pre-wrapped and fresh. The suits became a grey blur against the counter. But eventually they tailed off, returning to their jobs, homes and shopping sprees.

"Good job I came in. You guys were drowning in

here."

"Would've been even better if you'd been here from the start, Dude."

"Don't be a dick, Denver. Well, now I've saved your asses, I'm off. Places to be."

And as quick as she arrived, Jenny was gone, the ember of her cigarette disappearing in the winter gloom.

"Man, she is so hot," said Denver.

"If you say so."

"Listen man, I've got somewhere to be too. You mind if I scoot?"

"Why not? You normally do."

"You're a pal. See you tomorrow."

I DON'T MIND it so much, the cleaning. It's kind of cathartic. And after the mental rush of the day, seeing the coffee house quiet rounds things off nicely. I think I'd like to live here. Not as a coffee house, obviously. But replace the front windows with a normal house front, and the inside is kind of perfect. The counter would be where the living room is, up a few steps at the back to the dining room. Who doesn't want a spiral stairway to their bedroom? And I'd leave the heater above the door so I could see Natalie's jig when she came to visit.

Realising I was treading on stalker territory, I scratched that last part.

I cleaned the Brasilia first because it's the worst job. Both espresso handles, the steam nozzle, under the drainage area. Leave everything upside down to dry. Balancing cup within cup within cup like a ceramic spine, and holding a stack of plates in the other hand, I could clear most of the crockery in one go. I'm pretty sure I left the table by the window on purpose, but I wasn't aware of it at the time.

A ring of fossilized cappuccino ran around the inside of her cup, a little dip where Natalie's lip had been. I could smell her. Now the coffee was gone, the scent was as clear as if I were seeing her. I stood for a moment and placed the smells. There was no perfume, just the scent of clean skin. Pheromones, of course, that tickled parts of me I'd rather not discuss. Peppermint and Mountain Fresh; questions answered. Her lip gloss had been cherry and earlier in the day she'd eaten…chocolate orange. Probably just one piece.

I stood there for an embarrassing amount of time before shaking myself.

On my way back to the kitchen, I growled. I have many growls, although I never know when to expect one. They come from somewhere I'm not really in tune with. Some are like purring, others only come when I get…excited. But the growl that came on my way to the kitchen was one I very rarely heard.

Directly opposite the counter where I'd worked all day, there was a small table. One chair. Put there because Michelle, the manager, can't stand the thought of missing a single potential customer. We call it the Loner Station. Not very original, I know, but that chair attracts a certain type of customer. The kind without friends, colleagues, or any other human being who's willing to be in their vicinity. And it was the Loner Station that the growl didn't like.

Moving closer, I eventually smelled what my subconscious had.

A musk; thick with a sharp edge that made my eyes pinch. Like wet dog.

No guide dogs had been in. There had been a tramp but Denver chased him out with the mop. I pretended not to care as I snatched an empty sandwich packet from the table. Corned Beef. Three slices of tomato had been thrown back into the wrapper.

I checked the windows, locked the door and rattled the shutters down, all while definitely not thinking about that smell.

✕

ANOTHER COFFEE HOUSE battle had been fought. Denver carried himself off like Russell Crowe, and I was left sweeping up the man-bits and torn loincloths.

Metaphorically speaking.

The dishwasher rattled and gurgled. I leant against the counter, waiting for the little blue button to turn green. I was a bit on edge. It was that smell. It wasn't there anymore, thankfully. A day of swarming bodies and good dose of air-freshener had destroyed it, but I kept looking at that chair and wringing my memory for a face or even a loose description. My nerves were so frayed that when the *jingle-ingle* of the door rang, I leapt a mile.

I span around, ready for anything. Except Natalie.

"Hi," she said.

"Oh, hi. Urm, we're closed. Sorry."

I thumbed at the Brasilia, in pieces, dribbling suds.

She dipped her chin, and I think I saw a thin line of tears against her mascara. She must have had a real java-addiction.

"Oh."

"Sorry."

"No problem."

I let her get all the way to the door before my brain kicked in.

"But if you don't mind ordinary coffee, we have some instant out back."

It was an old jar of low-cost decaf. I had to use the spoon to break off enough of the solidified mass to serve us both. And since the dishwasher refused to finish, I had to make do with a couple of old mugs from the back of the cupboard. One had a chip out of the rim, probably Denver's fault. I gave her the other one.

"Sorry about this," I said, offering her the cup without a chip. "If it's any consolation it's free of charge."

She smiled, but just sniffed the coffee rather than tasting it.

We stood across the counter from each other, holding our old mugs like grails, or maybe shields.

"I'm Natalie, by the way. Nat."

"Stephen. Steve. Or, Phen, if you like." God bless her, she actually laughed. She looked like she needed it. "Shall we sit down? Up at the back? I've already cleaned up there."

Setting my cup down, I went and locked the door. Nat hawked me the whole way.

"Just so we don't get any more customers. That was the last of the shitty coffee. Sorry, I didn't mean to say shitty. Shit."

She just shook her head.

"Sit down, Phen."

I sank down onto the chair.

"So, you didn't come in at lunch," I said.

"You noticed?"

"Well, you know, we have to take care of our

regulars."

"I wasn't in work today. Family thing. How's your hand? It looked like it hurt."

Taking her change of subject as a sign, I showed her the back of my un-bandaged paw.

"Not a scratch. Just stung a bit. You know, not as bad as it looked."

That small snatch of conversation, and the silences in between, took long enough that her coffee had a skin on top.

"Thanks," she said, and got up to leave.

"Urm, hold on a second."

She did.

I hadn't planned on that, and had nothing to follow with. She must have noticed, because she bailed me out. Through the coffee house's glass front, the sun was long gone. She looked out at the premature night for a minute before asking:

"Do you want to walk me to my bus?"

"Yeah. That'd be…yeah. Just hold on a minute."

The dishwasher's button winked green. I stabbed it, opened the door to a plume of steam and pulled out the drawer.

"Don't you need to dry those?" Nat asked.

"Nah. I'm the first in tomorrow. They can wait."

"First one in, last one out. You must be dedicated."

"I think the word you're looking for is 'Mug'."

"Chipped or non-chipped?" She smiled.

Lights off, door locked, shutters down, and we were out in the night. Together.

The shop fronts were dark voids with half-seen shapes hiding inside. Only a few streetlamps cast amber pools at stupid distances apart. Wheelie bins and rubbish bags had been brought out into the street, making rock formations in the dark. I had to choke back the smell of refuse, swallowing frequently.

Her little hand, tucked into its mitten, slid through my arm.

"Do you mind?"

"Not at all."

"I hate this time of year," she said. "You get to work in the dark, come home in the dark. There's a deficiency, you know. Something you get from sunlight that makes you miserable if you don't get it."

"Vitamin D. That's why that drink's called Sunny D."

"Really?"

"I have no idea if that's true."

I laughed, and she squeezed my arm. All of a sudden, my ribs felt heavy.

A thud. Something slamming into the ground loud enough to echo from the shop fronts. The rattle of a pop can avalanche followed like gunfire. Nat grabbed my arm, sinking in to me. I squeezed back. I think I was more glad of her than she was of me.

I could see where the cans spilled out onto the ground and into a puddle of lamplight. But the rest was too dark. Over the smell of rotting rubbish, I caught something else. I stiffened, and Nat felt it.

"What is it?"

"Nothing," I lied. "Let's go this way."

There was a small street to our right, more of an alley, with a pub that only opened Thursday nights. Beyond the alley was a glimpse of the main road, the odd car hushing by. Further was the church, its gothic face lit from below like a child telling ghost stories. We'd have to go through the church grounds, and it would take longer to reach the bus station, but there was no way I wanted to walk past the fallen bin now. Not with that sweaty musk making my nostrils flare. Before we reached the end of the alley, a breeze carried another whiff of it toward me. It was in front, not behind.

A growl in the dark.

"Steve, was that you?"

"No," I said, sounding too surprised for my own liking.

I had to strain to see him. Like an optical illusion where you have to blur your eyes to reveal the secret. A grey coat flapped at his ankles. Deep creases and whispy stubble made distorting patterns of light and shadow across his face. He was pissing in the gutter. As we watched him, he limped across the alley and pissed on the other side too. Steam rose from the spreading trickle.

Nat thrummed like a plucked guitar string. I tried to stop myself shaking too, but her vibration seemed to carry through me.

He was breathing too fast. I didn't like it. *Huff-huff-huff* steaming from his nose and mouth like opium smoke. And when he spoke, the vapour coiled out past narrow teeth.

"Winter soon," he said. The sound of a zip. "Nights drawing in. First snow on its way."

I didn't reply. He nodded as if I had.

"It'll be a cold one."

The conversation caught me off guard. Commenting on the weather was the last thing I expected.

His head tilted to the side, dry lips pursed as if he were sucking a mint. I wasn't sure if he was listening, or thinking.

"Ba-dumba-dumba-dum," he said. "Scared or excited, boy?"

I couldn't help the growl. Nat tried desperately to occupy the same space as me, but didn't register the sound. He heard it, and his smile faded. He nodded again.

"Spring seems a long way off," he said.

I shrugged at him, opening my hands in a 'so

what' gesture.

He went from standing to full sprint in a blink. I was in the air and hitting the tarmac before I could register what happened. Pain shot up through my spine, knocking the wind out of me. Nat was on her backside in front of the stranger. His eyes were on me. I didn't move. He snorted. Reaching down to Nat, he dragging her up by the jacket. She whimpered as her feet kicked air and then set down. He shook her at me, showing me that he had her.

Shuffling up to my haunches, I stayed still. It was there, right behind my eyes, tearing at itself in an effort to be released. It knew, as well as I did, what he was. Another, like me, not like me. My teeth ground together until the gums bled. Tasting blood made the wolf howl in my head.

He shook her again until she screamed a little.

"I'll do it," he said. Nat was off the ground now, held up like a puppet. As a show of strength, it wasn't very good. He was struggling to hold her, having to overbalance to keep her up. He was old, weak.

Nat's feet lashed out, catching him on the flank. He cursed as his leg buckled and Nat scuttled clear.

I was up, darting to the side, grabbing a wheelie bin and whipping it from the ground. With a hollow plastic drumbeat, he was swiped off his feet. He hit the alley wall with a wet *thwack*, surrounded by splintered plastic. Rubbish was everywhere. He lay there for a moment. I thought it was over. He looked beaten already.

But again his speed surprised me. Jerking up, he cannoned into my stomach and we fell together.

He was stronger now, willing to let out more of the beast than I would with Nat nearby. He tore at my clothes, cuffing me around the head with glancing blows. That damp smell came out of him in condensed clouds and now there was piss and garbage mixed with it. My stomach rolled as we grappled. I tried to grab at his waist and realized how little of him there was beneath that old coat. Stars wheeled beyond his head, and I thought they were falling until the breeze drew the glistening flecks into eddies. The first flurries of snow wound around us as we brawled on the alley floor. A breeze blew the thickening flakes across us.

The blows stopped.

The stranger looked up at the sky. His eyes glistened in their darkened sockets.

"No, not yet," he whispered.

When he looked back to me, his eyes were a soft yellow. Grabbing my jacket, he slammed me against the ground.

"Come on," he snarled. "Come on!"

My fist ground into his hip like a pestle in mortar. He screamed with a grind of the wasted joint and

I shoved up hard. He fell away, holding himself and whining. Dragging myself to my feet, I went after him. But he wasn't even watching me. His face was turned up to the sky. Flakes melted on his sunken cheeks.

I finally heard Nat, who could have been shouting me for an age. She was saying my name, and now tugging at me.

"Please. Please, let's go."

The stranger was looking to me again. His wide pupils were a cataract grey.

"No," he said. "Please don't."

"Come *on*, Steve," snapped Nat. I let her pull me away.

The stranger lashed out. He caught my jeans leg in with pale knuckles.

"I'm not done," he said. "Don't leave me."

Nat aimed a kick at him but didn't connect.

We half ran, half stumbled up to the road and over. I looked back, and felt sick for it. The stranger was still there, laid on the alley floor, curling himself against the snow that settled on his coat.

Around a set of bent and jagged railings we found ourselves in the church yard. Weaving between a pair of floodlights we finally slowed down.

"What the hell was that?" asked Nat.

I knew this was where the explanations had to come. This was how it always was, they always found out at least some of it, and there was no good way of explaining.

"I-"

"Mad. Absolutely mad. I swear, this town gets worse," she said. "You can't even walk to a bus without getting accosted by some pissed-up old creep. Hey, you're shaking, are you ok?"

"Um, yeah. I'm fine."

She threw herself around me and we nearly fell over.

"I'm so glad you were there."

"Glad?"

"Of course! I can't imagine what would have happened if that old bastard had got me on my own."

"Well, yeah, I guess. Are you hurt?"

"Just a bump, but you must be in agony. He went crazy. How are you really feeling?"

Tearing off her gloves, her fingers were on my face and in my hair. I closed my eyes as she checked for blood.

"Wow, I think you're ok."

"Oh, I'm not so sure. Maybe you should check again."

She smiled.

"I don't want to hang around here. Let's go."

THE VENDING MACHINE barfed out a pair of thick

drinks that might have been coffee. We didn't drink them anyway. Sat on the bus terminal bench the paper cups made good hand warmers. The snow was falling for real now. With each bus that came and went, there was more snow on their windscreens and roofs.

There didn't seem much to say. Now and again she'd huff and shake her head. I asked if she was ok. She cried a little, and I sat useless beside her. Eventually the coffee was cold and we went to find a bin in a binless station.

She missed her bus three times or more for the sake of sitting in silence. I squeezed her hand once, and she squeezed back, but when she used it to brush her hair aside, I didn't reconnect.

Another 70A pulled in and the doors hissed open.

"I should really go," she said. "These buses don't run all night."

"Yeah. Let's avoid any *Casablanca* moments, eh?"

"I promise not to go Hollywood on you."

"Here love, you getting on, or what?" asked the bus driver.

I must have been pulling some puppy-dog face because she was smiling again.

"Yep," she answered, and left me stood there. I watched her hand over the exact change and take her ticket. I watched her pick a seat, and the bus pulled away. Rounding the corner, it was finally out of sight.

I bounded out into the snowstorm. A grey tunnel of flakes rushed toward me as I sped back the way we'd come. Across the graveyard, I vaulted the railing and was over the road in a moment, just in time to miss Natalie's bus as it drove by.

The alleyway had been cleansed white. Piles of bin bags and wheelie bins were snowmen waiting to happen. Flakes like five-pence pieces filled the air. Where the stranger had laid was a hollow but it wouldn't be there much longer. Stooping low over the depression, there was no scent. The air was too fresh from the snow. Only a trail of small prints led out of the alleyway. I didn't follow although the odd scuffed print from a dragged paw would make it so easy. I knew the stranger's end would be coming soon, even without my help.

Oestrids

C HRIS ROLLED AWAY from the stream of sunlight leaking through the curtains. Finding Emma, he kissed her nose and plucked a string of hair from her cheek. His feet clenched the carpet and he stretched before tugging on his pyjama bottoms. Somewhere beyond the curtains, a wood pigeon hooted without end, just like every damn morning since the world was created as far as Chris could tell. One of these days, that pigeon was going to get it. Chris checked the doormat and found no mail. He smiled at himself, shaking his head. The kettle made a noise as if choking on phlegm, spewing steam, and clicked. The tea itself tasted sharp. The kettle needed descaling.

Sitting at the breakfast table, Chris stared at the table top until the tears started. Pale droplets hit the wood, spreading out and joining together until there was a pool of saltwater. He cried until his tea cooled and the sun began to warm the air around him. He cried until the wood pigeon went home and the beam of light from the kitchen window slid across the floor tiles.

When that was done he showered but it was cold. Filling a bowl with water, he took a towel and flannel back into the bedroom. Emma was exactly where he'd left her, one hand up by her face, the other across her body. He set the bowl down on the bedside table and lifted her arm to peel back the sheets. When he got to her waist, he stopped for a moment, dreading that It would still be there, and dreading that It wouldn't. Holding his breath, he tugged again. Just like Emma, it hadn't moved.

The flaccid sac spread out behind her, now the size of a dinner plate. The main tendril still wrapped across Emma's waist, burying itself into her abdomen and spreading beneath her skin with a hundred little green branches.

Chris turned away, wetting the flannel and squeezing it out. He stroked Emma's hair aside, dabbing at her face. The sac made a noise. Clacking like a bicycle wheel. He didn't have to look, but he knew it was shivering; sucking the water through Emma like a sponge.

"Shut up, you," he said, and carried on with his task.

It took an hour or more to clean every inch of his

wife without moving her, patting her dry and combing her hair, and the whole time the sac clacked and shivered.

SCISSORS, THE SALAD tongs, the sharpest knife he could find. The cricket bat. Chris eyed his tools laid in the road, his legs crossed under him just by the white line. From force of habit, he checked for traffic again, and laughed at himself.

The dog lay a few inches in front of him. Its back leg twitched as if dreaming, just like Emma's eyes would flutter, but it wasn't moving. It had its own sac like an anchor on the tarmac. Smaller, but the same. He reached out with the tongs, sliding one edge under the sac. Its skin rippled, not slick but not dry, enough like rubber to be from a joke shop, enough like skin to be alive. The sac clacked; clacked louder. The ripples travelled along the tendril in pulses, moving the dog's skin. The dog panted shallow, its chest pumping faster and faster.

Chris drew back the tongs. The dog settled. The clacking stopped.

There was an obvious place to start. And if it didn't work, there were the Powells next door to practice on, and the Joneses after that, and on and on until he got this right. He snatched the scissors from the tarmac, slipping his fingers into the rings. The blades slid under and over the tendril, but didn't touch. Just like playing Operation.

Don't set off the bell. Don't kill the patient. The dog. Your wife.

Snapping the blades together, he sliced the cord like freeing a baby from its mother. Chris fell back, hands pressed to his ears. The sac was screeching, loud enough to cause dark flecks in his vision. The dog thrashed, legs in the air as if scratching its back on the road until blood darkened the tarmac. Foam lined its mouth, the tongue hung out between the teeth like a tendril of its own. The sac screeched on. Chris rolled away, certain he was screaming but he couldn't hear himself. Finding the cricket bat, he scurried forward. The sac exploded with the force of the blow, spraying a thick red fluid into the road, splattering Chris' shirt and face. He vomited in the Powells' rose bushes.

CHRIS SAT IN a chair beside the bed. The curtains thrown open, sunlight caressed Emma's slumbering body, making it glow. The sac laid out of sight, basking in her cool shadow. It was bigger again, like a deflated beach ball made of skin, but from here he couldn't see it and the sunlight's haze almost hid the tendril entirely. He sat for most of the day, watching his wife take a summer nap. Eventually he moved over to her, running his hand over her shoulder, stroking her hair, spreading her fingers with his own before locking them together.

JESSICA POWELL CURLED on her side, knees squeezing her large stomach and sagging breasts together into a single mass. Her hair was tied back, a single block of silver that tugged at her temples until her wrinkles were almost stretched flat. The tendril entered her pitted buttock, climbing up near her spine like a hidden hose pipe. James Powell laid on his back, head tilted, still snoring with each breath weeks after he went to bed. His sac was under the covers, entering through his groin.

Chris stood by the bed feeling like a burglar, a trespasser, a psychopath with his little bag of tools. He'd buried the dog yesterday and gone home to Emma. He'd slept on his plan. Then this morning he'd reread the encyclopaedias, making sure he understood what needed to be done. Because he had a theory. And surgery wasn't the way to go. The sacs were parasitic. Like tapeworm. So to starve the sac, he had to starve the host. He stood by Jessica, but simply couldn't, so he moved around to her husband. He pinched James' nose, smiling when the snoring changed pitch. How many times had he played this game? James falling asleep in the sun at some summer barbeque, Chris sneaking over to grab James' nose and set him snorting. The first barbeque of the year would have been weeks ago if not for the sacs. Chris' face collapsed. He closed his eyes, and reached over to cover his neighbour's mouth.

A few minutes later, Chris pressed a cold towel to his eye. James had fought back, just like the dog, although never waking. His hand had come up so fast that Chris didn't see it. Reeling, Chris had to reapply his smothering hands and just take the blows that James dealt out. The sac had screeched, of course, but hadn't let go of James. Not when he thrashed, not when his body grew tired and heavy, not even when he was dead.

Chris dug into his bag, arraying the ingredients on the bed beside Jessica's sac. Salt, bleach, weed killer, a small box of rodent poison. Chris still wasn't sure if the sacs were plant or animal and he wasn't going to leave any option untried. He took the salt first. But why? Surely the bleach would kill what salt would, and faster. Because he was enjoying himself, that's why. Every sac he killed, he got a little jolt. It was like playing doctor, guerrilla warrior and God all in one go. And the Powells? Casualties of his own private crusade.

He sprinkled on the salt, only the first layer in the sac's torture. What he wanted was little areas of creeping dryness, dark patches of death and the sac to screech again. He knew he was really pissing them off when they screeched. But the sac didn't shrivel like a slug. It sat there with a light coating of white particles and did nothing.

Chris pulled the bleach from his bag. He unscrewed the child-lock cap on his second try and drizzled sink-cleaner onto the sac like salad dressing. The salt melted into the growing puddle, spreading out the grains. But nothing else. Not a shudder, no clack or screech.

"Smug little bastard," he said, jumping at the sound of his own voice. He clapped a hand across his mouth. His eyes snapped to Jessica. Then he laughed. She wasn't going to wake up. He could perform cabaret in his underwear and the sac would keep her asleep.

Still shaking his head, he retrieved a towel from the Powell's bathroom and dabbed the sac dry. This had to be scientific. He shouldn't mix what he was testing. Otherwise how'd he know what really worked? Tapping the sac like drying a baby's bottom, Chris muttered to himself to fill the silence he hoped would be broken by now.

"Hope these aren't your best towels, Jessica. Hope this little bastard is worth ruining them."

Now, how did rat poison work?

In a world that still had wars and crime and traffic jams, there had been a little boy. It was another town, several decades distant. And that little boy, who looked something like Chris, had a dog. He was a Westie, a West Highland Terrier, and black like a streak of coal that ran around and pissed when excited. He was called Oscar, and the little boy who looked something like Chris had loved him very much. The house, decades away and silent as any other now, had rats. Oscar loved to chase them and he'd spend hours in the garden yapping at bushes and digging for tunnels. But the little boy's father was sick of the rats, and he decided to do something about it. So he put down poison. All round the garden, in the gutters where the rats would run, and under the bushes. Oscar had to stay inside. He sat in the window, watching for the rats, his little tail wagging.

And eventually, he got out.

Chris could remember exactly how Oscar looked when he came home from school. Laid on the patio in a pool of his own blood that seemed to make the little dog glisten. Flies were on him already; in a cloud above and a crawling mass below. Chris screamed.

But Little Chris learned something that day that might save his wife years later when the sacs came; might even save the world. You had to eat rat poison. It was a blood thinner, making the rats bleed internally until they expired just like Oscar. But the sac had no mouth or nose or anywhere else to stuff the poison. So, it became Jessica's job to deliver the final dose. Chris slid the rubber gloves on. He sprinkled the poison onto a bowl of water, stirring, and then wet the flannel just like he had done with Emma that morning. He squeezed the water onto Jessica's back where the tendril undermined her skin. The sac clacked and shook and the water disappeared into the old woman's pores. So far so good.

Chris sat back to wait.

Nothing. Not a damn thing. The sac had soaked up the water, filtering out the poison and probably left it in Jessica's body to do more harm there. Little bastard.

But the sac started to make a sound he'd never heard before. A rattle, like someone breathing through a mouthful of phlegm. Like James' snoring before his neighbour smothered him. Something had worked. Something was happening. The blisters came quicker than Chris thought they would, lifting the sac's membranes in little clear bubbles that soon began to turn a deeper red. Chris' back bumped against the wall before he realised he was backing away. The blisters swelled, joining together into one large bubble of fluid. The sac's rattling was getting louder and It shuddered like a broken-down bus. Chris retreated into the Powell's en-suite bathroom and watched through a crack in the door. The sac's skin was rising like a kiddy's paddling pool filled with blood; the blisters getting darker and darker as the skin was stretched thin.

Chris fell back. Something hit the door with a sound like a water balloon-collision. He laid on the tiles for a while, waiting for some other sound. Easing the door open, he looked out into the blood bath. Thin trickles of sac blood decorated every surface; the inside of the window, the vanity mirror and both of the Powells' bodies. The sac was now a stain, and slivers of thick membrane dotted around the room.

"Fuck me."

And then he said it again, shouted it, when Jessica Powell rolled over.

The old woman turned toward him, sluggish, rubbing her eyes. She saw her dead husband, the sac buried in his back, then the blood-strewn room and the familiar madman beside her. She screamed, and started to scramble up the bed until she was upright. Chris darted forward, trying to explain through the noise but soon moved away again. Jessica's voice was becoming wet as if she were gargling mouthwash. Her eyes, like dinner plates, grew dark as the blood vessels burst. Soon it was streaming down her face; from her ears and between her teeth. It spread between her legs and even from the beds of her fingernails as they grabbed the bed clothes. Her spine spasmed, thrusting her gut and sagging breasts toward the ceiling.

Then she was quiet, and flaccid.

"Fuck me," Chris said again, if only for something to say.

ON THE UPSIDE, he knew the water delivery system worked. He could use it to try other poisons now and he had all the time in the world to test new concoctions. No, that wasn't true. He just didn't know how long he had, how long the sacs would grow and what would happen when they were done. It was just better not to think about it.

On the downside, his neighbours were dead. He'd killed them. But it was more manslaughter than murder, wasn't it? No, he'd definitely killed James on purpose. They were casualties of war, then. Understandable. When Emma woke and found their entire street dead in their beds at her husband's hand, she'd understand. Hell, she should be grateful. It was all for her.

Chris crumpled up the cereal box. It was the third one he'd had, stolen from a few houses down, and the flakes of wheat had been growing stale. Could it have been that long? He checked the sell by date and tried to remember the last time he knew what day it was. By the cereal box, it had been over a month. He laughed. It was Thursday today. He knew because the day before yesterday he got up half asleep and put the bin out for collection. That meant it should have been Tuesday. Of course, stood on the curb he'd realised no other bins were out and he'd taken it back in. No one was coming. Not for the bin, or to save him; not to take Emma to a secret government lab where they were experts in sac-removal. He was on his own.

He went upstairs to check on Emma, or rather to remind himself of what kind of world he lived in. While it had once been flat, the sac was now filling out like a popcorn carton on the grill. It had to be three inches deep already. He knelt beside it, resting his chin on the bed so he was eye to membrane with it.

"Level with me," he said. "What are you up to?"

When he got no answer, he prodded it, no longer caring that his hand wasn't covered up. The sac clacked but not as urgently as before.

"Ve has vays of making you talk."

Clack clack clack.

"Oh, so you sink you har being clever do you? Ve shall see, my friend. Ve shall see."

CHRIS STOOD IN another bedroom. The Jones' were dead, as were the Campbells and the Montoyas. He'd gone through so many of his neighbours that he was now at the point where he didn't know their names. That somehow made it harder. In these houses he couldn't just walk through, knowing his way to their bathrooms and stairways. He had to search, and that meant walking past the family photos, finding the little rodent corpses in their hamster cages, the cat with its own sac on the kitchen worktop. But he always killed the animals first. No, he experimented with them. No, he definitely killed them. He didn't expect anyone to survive his probing, who was he kidding? And who was there to answer to? When he found something that worked, he'd save Emma, then there would be others, and soon a hundred dead people in Yorkshire would be acceptable casualties in the saviour of mankind. He'd have a statue, and their names would be little brass plaques at his feet.

Humming the national anthem because he couldn't remember the words, Chris took out his spray bottle and subjected the nameless neighbour to his latest concoction.

Minutes later, he stood in front of the bathroom mirror scrubbing at his face and hands to remove the sac's vile blood. As he scrubbed, the tears came again, drawing lines through the gore like pale scratches. His teeth squeezed together until his gums ached; fingernails bit into palms. With the heels of his shaking hands against his temples he felt the pound of his arteries. He was shaking like a leaf, like a wet dog, like a sac. He was distantly aware of a keening sound, a high-pitched, wordless whine; when he realised it was coming from him, he didn't bother to stop.

CHRIS FOUND THE man laid on the pavement only a few streets away from his house. The sac entered the leg of his shorts, bloated to a pulsing dome, just like the others. What had once been an early morning newspaper in the man's hand had been reduced to pulp by some forgotten rain storm. The skin across the backs of his arms and neck leading up to his bald crown were brown to almost black. When Chris lifted his wrist, the underside was still pale. So many days in the sun had made the man a penguin. Chris laughed and his voice carried down the street and away like an unstrung kite. The sac clacked when its host was moved, the sound was deeper than when this had all started, as if the bastards had gone through puberty.

Getting down on the ground, Chris could see how the man had fallen, breaking his nose on the tarmac and the blood had permanently stained the ground.

"Never even tried to stop yourself falling," said Chris. "Stupid bastard."

Jumping up, he pounded his boot into the man's ribs. Again and again until they cracked and blood leaked through his shirt.

"Stupid bastard! Stupid bastard!"

That sac squealed like a squashed frog so Chris drove his boot down on it, sending a corona of dark fluid spurting into the street.

STRAINED LIKE TEA through the kitchen curtains, the daylight filled Chris' kitchen with amber where dust motes drifted like pearls. The man at the table had once been a husband, a neighbour and a friend. He'd been a son but never a father. And now he was the last man on earth, sat at a small table in a silent house, silent street, silent town. And beyond that, the floating carcass of Britain's islands all as still as that single room. A glass of water sat on the table top in front of him, a thin scum on the surface. The smell of rotten food leaked from the open fridge and water crept across the floor.

Chris shifted his weight out of habit rather than comfort. Some part of his brain continued to protect him although his consciousness was elsewhere. Emma lay upstairs, beyond the bedroom door and beyond his help. When he woke this morning, he'd noticed the tiny wrinkles in the corners of her eyes for the first time. Only slight, but they hadn't been there before. Her ribs leaned out over her pitted stomach. Her knees jutted from her withering legs. And the sac lay beside her, the length of her leg now, and solid. Cracks were forming on its thickened hide, like Emma's wrinkles, scoring its body into segments. And it pulsed. Stretched. Throbbed like an insect heart. Whatever was going to happen was happening soon. And there was nothing he could do to stop it.

So Chris sat in the kitchen. He slept with his head on the tabletop and breathed because he didn't know how to stop. And he waited.

Even through the ceiling, he could hear the slow clack, the sound the sac now made day and night without end like the torturous drip of water driving its way into his mind until he pre-empted every sound with a twitch of his eye.

Then there was the crack. Just one. A dull sound like the popping of wood on a fire. If Chris had been moving before, he froze. His lungs halted and his heart seemed to whisper so it wasn't found.

A soft thud; the sound of something hitting the bedroom floor.

Chris turned his face up to the ceiling, his body screaming that he needed to breathe.

And there was the sound of the bedroom door, dragging across the carpet.

Not Before Bed

'M OUTSIDE YOUR bedroom door.

Go take a look if you like. It will only take a second.

Nothing? But as soon as it clicks to the jamb, I'm there. My toes curling in your carpet, inches from your door.

As you change, as you turn out the light. I'm there. As you slide down into your linen cocoon, I'm there. I'm patient. I can wait.

I press my serrated ear to the wood panelling. I can hear you breathe. I listen as you turn over, shifting your drowsy weight into that familiar position.

Your breathing slows.

I've listened to you for a long time, I know when you're asleep. And when you are, I slip inside.

You are fascinating to me, you creatures that sleep. I lay on your chest and breathe in your scent.

Oh, you sleep on your side? I like that better. Then I can squirm up behind you, fold myself to match your form. Sometimes you feel my breath on your neck, or fingernails brushing your hair. But you won't wake. I won't let you.

Slumber on as I lay beside you and sing soft nightmares in your ear. I know when you're dreaming; I can smell it.

When you mumble in your sleep, I'm the one who answers. When sweat prickles from your tormented dreams, I'm the one who licks the brine from your skin. And when you open your eyes, and can't move, it's the fear of me that freezes you. It's the fear of me that halts the voice in your fragile throat.

But you get some sleep.

I'll see you tomorrow.

Thank you for reading *Not Before Bed*.

Other books by this author

Greaveburn

A Hero murdered. A Girl alone. A city of Villains.

From the crumbling Belfry to the Citadel's stained-glass eye, across acres of cobbles streets and knotted alleyways that never see daylight, Greaveburn is a city with darkness at its core. Gothic spires battle for height, overlapping each other until the skyline is a jagged mass of thorns.

Abrasia, the rightful heir, lives as a recluse in order to stay alive. With her father murdered and her only ally lost, Abrasia is alone in a city where the crooked Palace Guard, a scientist's assistant more beast than man, and a duo of body snatchers are all on her list of enemies.

Under the cobbled streets lurk the Broken Folk, deformed rebels led by the hideously scarred Darrant, a man who once swore to protect the city. And in a darkened laboratory, the devious Professor Loosestrife builds a contraption known only as The Womb.

With Greaveburn being torn apart around her, can Abrasia avenge her father's murder before the Archduke's letter spells her doom.

The Adventures of Alan Shaw

Escaping the workhouse was only the beginning of Alan Shaw's adventures.

For an orphan growing up on the streets of Victorian London, staying alive is a daily battle filled with choices a child should never have to make. Then Alan is offered more money than he can imagine; enough to take him to the new world and a new life. He only has to do one thing first – something that could bring the British Empire to a grinding halt.

In a series of adventures that take him from sea to sky, from Brighton to Bombay, Alan grows up in a steam-driven era where Automatons walk the streets of London and dirigibles master the air. Pitted against mad alchemists, tentacled submersibles, bomb-wielding saboteurs and the apocalyptic cult of the Ordo Fenris, Alan has his work cut out for him.

With a past as dark as his, who knows what Alan might grow up to be?

Lightning Source UK Ltd.
Milton Keynes UK
UKOW01f1213160916

283153UK00002B/6/P